LABOR OF LOVE
J. K. Winn

www.BOROUGHSPUBLISHINGGROUP.com

LABOR OF LOVE
Copyright © 2019 J.K. Winn

ISBN 978-1-951055-42-4

To all my adoring and adorable children and their spouses,
Jonah, Chris, Leah, Brian, Aaron, and Gina.

I could not have persevered and accomplished what I have without
your love.
Thank you for bringing such joy into my life.

ACKNOWLEDGMENTS

To the many friends, family, writers, and readers who have shown me support and encouragement over the years. I'm especially grateful for the guidance and direction I received from the late Marion Jones and the San Diego Chapter of the Romance Writer's of America. I could never have done this without all of you. And finally, a big shout out to my critique partners, Ann and Judith, and my fellow writers, Janice MacDonald and Sylvia Mendoza who offered their wisdom and experience.

LABOR OF LOVE

Chapter 1

Water. Cool, clear water. *Agua es vida*: A perfect blend of hydrogen and oxygen with the power to give life—or take it away.

Elena crouched down by the babbling brook and watched as the sun's rays skittered across its sparkling surface. She dipped a hand in, breaking surface tension and allowed the water to lick through splayed fingers. *How giving and forgiving water could be.*

She really should have been on her way back to town, but for a moment she cupped a hand, brought it close to her face for inspection. The water looked innocuous enough—refreshing really. It was hard to imagine it could be deadly. With sun beating down on her and moisture beading her brow, she had the sudden desire to take a sip and quench her thirst, but, as she knew, looks could be deceiving. This innocent-looking pool might be more dangerous than it appeared.

It might even be poisonous.

***

Bright sunlight glared through the windshield of Adam's Jeep Cherokee, momentarily blinding him. He pulled down the visor, but it didn't help. Neither did the suspicion that he was lost. Frustrated, he made a sharp right turn onto a side road and immediately regretted the move. The car jolted and bumped over deep tracks. The air conditioner all but useless, Adam swiped at his brow with the back of his hand. Moisture trickled down the back of his shirt.

Sheer stubbornness kept him driving down the road for a mile or two. When the road ran out, he pulled to the side and lifted the map from the passenger's seat. One dirt road and farm field looked pretty much like the next. How long since he'd left the main road? Where the hell was he? More to the point, why had he taken this damn assignment to Vandasillo in the first place?

I'm where I need to be, he told himself. *Where I've got to be unless I want to blow the opportunity of a lifetime.* Adam tapped his fingers on the steering wheel. Okay, no option, he had to turn back. He put the car in reverse and hit the gas. The wheels rumbled as they spun in a cloud of dust. As he shifted into drive, he spotted a woman. A good-looking woman. Long black hair and—how could he not notice—provocatively swaying hips. Jeez. Out here in the middle of nowhere?

He drew up alongside her. "Hi. I'm a bit lost. Could you point the way to Vandasillo?"

She watched him through wary eyes, the flicker of a nervous smile playing across her full lips. "It's straight ahead." She pointed toward a rise in the road. "Beyond that hill, you'll see another road. Make a left and it will take you into town."

Adam held her glance for a moment longer than he probably should have. "Thanks." He saluted the woman before continuing in the direction she recommended, toward an appointment with the unknown.

***

At her social service office in a dusty renovated barn on the outskirts of the small farming community of Vandasillo, Elena watched migrant workers with bent, tortured backs pluck juicy tomatoes from gnarled vines and place them in open wooden crates. Beyond the workers, rows of vibrant green plants extended for as far as the eye could see. Elena knew the drill: the endless hours of backbreaking work, the bruised and bleeding fingers, the sweltering heat. She had helped her parents pick crops when the family first arrived in the United States from Nicaragua.

Maria Ortega thrust a pudgy finger at Elena's face. "Are you listening to me?" She jerked the same finger in the direction of the workers. "Those people will die if something is not done soon."

"Take a seat. We need to talk." Elena motioned the distraught woman toward a chair, but she refused to sit.

Maria's free hand clutched the strap of a purse held against the floral print shirtwaist covering her protruding belly. "I tell you, two of my neighbors on Valley Road have been diagnosed with cancer—a cancer of the blood. Two. We have never had a case of this cancer

8

before, except for old man Madeira, and now two on one block. Explain that to me." Maria took a step closer to Elena. "And then the Olivas family gives birth to a baby with a heart that doesn't pump. *Dios mio*. What will become of us?"

"Could the doctors save the baby?"

Maria scowled. "They could do nothing."

Elena glanced down at the speckled linoleum floor. "I'm so sorry to hear that."

"It is the power plant," Maria said. "I am sure of it. Since it has been here, the riverbed, it smells funny, especially after a rain. You would know if you had not gone away."

Elena cringed inwardly. While Maria was more direct than others in the community, they all seemed to disapprove of her settling in Los Angeles after social work school. They had expected her to return to Vandasillo immediately upon graduation and thought she, like others before her, had forsaken them for the glamour and riches of big city life.

Now that she was back, she had to clear up any misunderstanding. She had worked hard, harder than most of her other classmates with English as their only language. Her primary purpose in gaining her degree was to help other migrant workers improve their lives.

Maria held out a hand to her. "I do not mean anything by what I say. What has possessed me lately? Since the pregnancy, I am scared. I already lost *un niño*. I do not want what happened to Lorena Olivas to happen to me. I do not want to lose this baby."

Elena took the outstretched hand in hers. "I'd probably feel the same way in your place."

Maria half-smiled for the first time that afternoon, revealing a missing tooth. "I know you have always done what you could for us. I do not know what Pablo and I would have done without you when he was sick and could not work." She reached over and bundled Elena up in a smothering hug against her belly. "We will always be grateful to you."

Elena breathed in the mixture of sweat and cheap perfume rising from Maria's skin. "I only did my job. And don't worry, I share your concerns. I plan to visit the power plant soon to find out if they have any part in all this "

With a sigh of relief, Maria released her.

"By the way, how's Pablo holding up? You never mentioned him."

Maria shrugged. "He is all right. Still complaining about that sore leg. He has not been able to spend too many hours in the field. We could use some help with the food bill."

"I'll see if you can get back on food stamps until he's better. Let's fill out the paperwork today."

"*Muchas gracias*." Maria signed the form that Elena handed her, then waddled out the door and into a faded yellow Volkswagen bug that sputtered and backfired as she drove away.

Elena closed the screen door to keep out a swarm of flies. She lifted the bottle of water she had collected on her walk by the stream and held it up to the light, still thinking over what Maria had said. She hoped it wasn't true that someone would knowingly or negligently taint the water, because it was almost too awful to contemplate. Not that she was naïve. She had experienced her share of deceit and inhumanity in her twenty-seven years, and she wouldn't be surprised if Maria's suspicions were validated. But it still perplexed her on some level how one human being could be so indifferent to the suffering of another.

Perhaps the increased incidence of cancer and birth defects might not be all that unusual in a growing community like Vandasillo, California, but it still seemed out of proportion to the number of residents. As the county social worker, her job included protecting the well-being of the community. Elena had to find out the truth.

***

A guardhouse secured the entrance to the Valley Hill Gas and Electric's Vandasillo plant, twenty-five miles outside of Fresno. The station served both Fresno and the surrounding towns. Behind it, huge chimneys belched out water vapor and smoke. Elena pulled her royal blue Toyota Tercel alongside the guardhouse. "I have an appointment with the plant manager at one."

The uniformed guard looked over a sheet pinned to a clipboard. "Elena Marquez?"

"That's right."

"Drive into the lot to your left and go up to the third floor. Mr. Rhoades's office is three-o-five. He's expecting you."

She followed his directions to the office. At a desk, a well-groomed young woman with hair brushed back in a knot looked up from her computer. "May I help you?"

Elena smiled down at the receptionist. "I have a one o'clock appointment with Mr. Rhoades."

The young woman studied her computer screen. "You must be Ms. Marquez. I'm sorry, Mr. Rhoades was called away for an unexpected meeting in Sacramento, but he asked me to have you speak with our attorney, Adam Slater. Here's his secretary's number." She held out a slip of paper. "Mr. Slater's in Los Angeles, but he'll be back on Thursday. You can arrange to see him then."

Elena stared at the note and felt a flare of anger. "But I had an appointment. I can't believe Mr. Rhoades would stand up an appointment without even a call."

The receptionist blushed. "It was unanticipated."

Elena swallowed her frustration. No use shooting the messenger. She held out her card. "Please give Mr. Rhoades my card and tell him I was here."

"I'll let him know."

Elena made her way back to her car, all the while watching two giant chimneys spew noxious smoke into the air. Suddenly suspicious, she knew she shouldn't have mentioned the real reason for her visit while setting up the appointment. But if Rhoades thought he was going to blow her off without an explanation, he had another think coming. As she turned the ignition key, the thump of the fuel pump mentally primed her persistence. She'd meet with Slater, all right, but she wasn't about to lie down and let any hotshot attorney from LA twist the truth.

She wanted answers, and she wanted them now.

Chapter 2

Elena leafed through a magazine in Adam Slater's sparsely furnished law office in a two-story old brick building, which housed a small law firm in the middle of town. She might as well have been reading Greek for all the attention she paid to the article. She had a job to do, and all she could think about was what she wanted to say and how to phrase it so she wouldn't alienate Slater before she had a chance to extract what she needed. She glanced at her watch for the hundredth time and looked up to spot the lost man from the week before striding into the room—the one who'd asked her for directions. A wide smile of recognition lit up his hazel eyes.

Weren't lawyers supposed to be starchy, white-haired types? If so, Slater wasn't your typical lawyer. She noted his navy-blue blazer, jeans and tooled boots. Thick wavy reddish-brown hair curled around his forehead, giving him a boyish look. She had to remind herself that he represented the power plant and his innocent appearance was deceptive.

"Elena Marquez?" He held out a card.

She nodded, glanced at the card. Gold lettering embossed woven ivory linen.

"It's *my* turn to point *you* in the right direction. Please come this way." He led her down the hall and stopped at an open door. "My office." Inside, by a walnut desk scattered with stacks of folders and a smattering of law books, he held one of two padded side chairs for her. "Please have a seat."

"Thank you."

He waited until she was seated, then settled into a black leather swivel chair on the opposite side of the desk. "Excuse the mess. I'm still moving in."

"I appreciate you seeing me on such short notice."

"No problem. As you might have guessed, I've arrived from Los Angeles and I have yet to fill my calendar with such stimulating reading as contracts and regulatory documents." His eyes met hers and something in them intrigued her as well as validated her sense that he wasn't another sleazy big-city lawyer.

She glanced around the office. A framed picture of a beautiful blonde on his desktop caught her eye. She wondered if the picture was of a relative, or perhaps his girlfriend.

"What can I do for you today?" he asked.

She wanted to get to the point. "There's been a rash of medical problems among the migrant workers in this part of the Valley. This month alone six people have been diagnosed with cancer, four with leukemia, and two couples have given birth to badly deformed children, one who died during delivery."

A frown creased his brow. "I'm sorry to hear that, but what does that have to do with Valley Hill Gas and Electric?"

"Eight incidents may not sound significant to you, but there are only five thousand or so people who regularly work these fields. Eight incidents in such a short time in such a small community seems suspect."

He shrugged. "I understand your concern, but I still don't see what this has to do with the power company."

"There's a rumor in the community that the river which irrigates the fields is being polluted by the power plant."

Adam placed a report in front of her. "The local plant manager, Harold Rhoades, asked me to show you this. As you can see"—he pointed at a grid with names of chemicals alongside numbers—"the most recent testing, less than a month ago, shows groundwater near the plant had no dangerous concentration of any toxic chemical. And why would they add chemicals to the water anyway? It doesn't add up."

"From what I understand, they keep the older pipes from corroding." Elena took the papers and rifled through them. "I need to study this more."

"Take your time." Adam rose and walked around the desk to the office door. "I'll be back in a few minutes."

Elena combed through the charts as thoroughly as she could within the time constraints of Slater's imminent return. According to the findings, chemicals had been found in the local groundwater at concentrations far below the toxic levels proscribed by the United States Environmental Protection Agency. The groundwater was safe to drink and use, the study concluded. She finished reading and sat pondering the report as Adam reentered the office.

"I read that before you came. It's obvious the power plant isn't the culprit in this case." He went over to a sink against one wall and poured tap water into two glasses. When he turned back, he held out a glass of water to her. "You must be thirsty in this heat. The water here has to be far safer than the treated liquid they pawn off on us in Los Angeles."

Obviously, he was trying to make a point with the tap water. She took the glass, but set it down on the desk blotter. "I read the report, and it sounds convincing, but it doesn't fully address the community's concerns."

Adam nodded and calmly sipped from his glass.

"I've done my homework," Elena said. "I know two examples of runoff from power plants that have caused similar problems in other communities. It seems that the by-products of fossil fuels, things like toluene or benzene, can be toxic to humans and animals at certain levels. They can create exactly what we're beginning to see here— an increase in cancers and birth defects."

He tipped his now empty glass in her direction. "You're obviously conscientious, but not necessarily on the right track. In the first place, I'm not even sure the number of cases you mentioned is out of the ordinary for a community this size, and even if they are, there's no evidence that ties these cases to the power plant."

"But the only study you've shown me was paid for by the company. How do you know it's unbiased and believable?"

He placed the glass on the desk with a thud. "Show me something that contradicts it. I have yet to see anything other than suspicion and hearsay. You're going to need a lot more than a couple of unrelated cancer cases to prove any responsibility on the part of a power company."

She sat forward. It would take every bit of her knowledge to contradict his argument. "The incidence of leukemia in the general population is six in every hundred thousand, which only serves to confirm my fears."

"Good point, if this was a normal population, but these people work day in and day out around fertilizers and other chemicals."

He had a good point, too. "Still, the way I was treated at the plant didn't exactly counteract my suspicions."

Slater flexed his brow. "What happened, Ms. Marquez?"

"Your friend, Harry Rhoades, stood me up for our scheduled appointment without any advance notice or explanation. That seems highly irregular."

Adam grinned. "I understand your confusion. When you made the appointment to meet with Rhoades, he didn't have any legal representation. I took the job only last week. I'm sure you're aware of the recent spate of legal cases in California against any company that deals with chemicals. The power plant decided to hire legal representation."

"That could be, but it could also be that Rhoades didn't dare deal with this himself because there's reason to avoid a confrontation."

"Why would you think that?"

"He may know something he's not telling you about the toxicity."

"That pretty dramatic, Ms. Marquez. Sounds like something in the tabloid news."

She bristled at his remark. "I don't read the tabloids, Mr. Slater. The incidence of suspicious illness is well documented."

"I can empathize with the concerns, but," he tapped the environmental report, "this verifies that we are not involved."

"I hope so, but I'm not going to accept this report at face value. I want you to know I'll continue to keep my eyes open." She studied her hands gripping the edge of his desk. "You know as well as I do that this population is ignored and overlooked. They are the forgotten people. For obvious reasons, they are suspicious of authority, and contrary to common wisdom, they are unable to secure the medical services they require beyond emergency care. They have no one to fight for them."

"Except for you."

"And now, it seems, I'm forced to fight you. Since hiring you at this time can't be coincidental. There must be more behind it than either of us know."

He made a face. "That sounds conspiratorial."

She stared him down. "Perhaps it is."

***

Adam had heard enough, even from a woman as appealing as Elena Marquez. "Is that all today? I have other things to attend to."

Elena lifted her glass. "You know the saying *agua es vida?*"

"Water is life?"

"It can be death, too. Let's hope this water isn't, but in case, I'll pass on it." She eyed a wilting spider plant on the edge of his desk. "Looks like that plant could use a drink more than I could." She emptied her glass into the pot.

He shook his head. "I admire you for being a strong person, Elena, and I can see you won't be easily convinced, but I don't believe you're barking up the right tree."

"Perhaps. But until I find out the truth, I'm going to keep on barking." She placed the glass down. "I'd like to ask a favor of you."

Adam eyed her. "And that would be?"

"Would you please convey my concerns to Rhoades?"

"Certainly."

"I'll probably never have the chance to speak with him myself. I'd like to hear what he has to say."

Adam reviewed the report. "Sure. Anything else?"

"Yes. I'm sure you spotted the water tank on the hill. It services all the fields in the area. I'd like you to meet me out there on Friday."

"For what?"

"I want to show you something that's important for you to see. Are you game?"

Adam glanced at his watch. He had planned to wrap this meeting up fifteen minutes earlier. Besides being terribly attractive, this woman was more sophisticated than he'd been led to believe. She was a worthy adversary, even if she was totally off track. "All right. I can do that."

***

Elena grabbed her appointment book from her briefcase leaning against Lorena's unstable chair. "I'll make a deal with you. If you do one thing for yourself this week, I'll meet with you." Lorena rubbed her puffy eyes. "I want you to go for a walk once a day, every day. I don't care where you go or how far, but I want you out of the house for as long as you can stand it."

Lorena stared past Elena and sighed. "*Si.*"

"Good." Elena made a note in the book, placed it back in her briefcase and rose. "I'll be back on Thursday afternoon. Will you be here?"

Lorena gave her a mirthless laugh. "*Si.*"

"I'll see you then." Elena made her way back to her office, more certain than ever after visiting Lorena that she was right pursuing the allegations against the power company. Even if the power company proved blameless, the investigation would motivate authorities to find the true source of the trouble.

At the office, she went through her mail and listened to the messages. After hearing a message from Maria Ortega about her water bill being too high, and then Jesse Hernandez's worry about his grandson's illness, Adam Slater's deep resonant voice filled her ears. "I was wondering what you were doing this Friday afternoon after we visit the water tank. Would you be able to show me one of those Sierra trails you mentioned? I'd sure like to know where to hike around here. Give me a call when you can."

Elena plopped into her chair and listened to the message a second time, surprised by her reaction. Instead of being annoyed at Adam's request, she was intrigued, which was annoying. She took a deep breath to bring her emotions under control. She couldn't allow them to drive her to do something she shouldn't, something that could be construed as a conflict of interest. Once she had followed similar feelings and they had led her into making a huge mistake. She was not about to make a second one on the rebound from the first.

She shrugged off any residual feelings about Adam's request before picking up the phone and calling him.

He answered on the second ring. "I was hoping it was you, Marquez. You got my message."

"Sure did, and I'd love to help you out, but I have to stop by my daughter Gabriella's class to meet with her teacher."

He cleared his throat. "But we'll be out by the water tank."

She tried to picture the disappointment on his face. She bet he wasn't a man well versed in letdowns. "I'm sorry. I don't think it's a good idea."

"You do realize this isn't intended to be a date. I wanted your help finding a good hiking trail. That's all."

She didn't realize anything of the sort and that's what intrigued and frightened her. "Of course, but I have a lot to do Friday. Perhaps you could head up to the National Park yourself and ask the ranger for advice."

Silence. Her heartbeat filled her ears.

He cleared his throat again. "All right, but if you free up any time, please let me know. I could really use your help to learn my way around the backcountry."

"Sorry." She hung up before she could change her mind. The temptation was far too dangerous.

She buried her head in a psychiatric report to dispel any thoughts of calling him back.

***

Adam pushed his chair back and interlocked fingers behind his head. The melody of Elena's perfectly pitched lilting voice still played in his head. How he enjoyed listening to her, if only she sung a different tune.

He'd hoped she would agree to his request. If he had the opportunity to spend time with her, he was certain he could convince her of the ridiculous nature of her militant stand against the power company and persuade her to ease up on them. But one thing she had yet to discover about him: he wasn't a quitter.

He might be deterred today, but he wasn't about to give up, not when he held the winning hand.

Chapter 3

The sunlight made Elena's long, straight, black hair shine while speckling her lavender shirt as they walked through the brush to the water tower. Adam paced her from behind, which gave him an up-close view of her fantastic ass. Unfortunately, he couldn't keep his eyes where he wanted them since the trail was narrow and steep, and he had worn his street shoes. He'd been so distracted by her curvy body, he'd neglected to put on the Nikes in his trunk.

Elena looked back at him. "Almost there."

"I still don't get why we're doing this."

She smiled. "You'll see."

He slid over pebbles and twigs, but caught himself before falling. He would be humiliated if she saw him stumble. "I sure hope the site is worth it." When they reached the tower, the sun was almost directly overhead. "What a way to spend our lunch hour. What do you do for dinner?"

She chuckled and pointed to a ladder on the side of the tower. "As an appetizer, let's climb."

He glanced down at his recently shined shoes. "You have to be kidding."

"Nope." She started up the ladder with ease. Clearly, she'd been here before. He followed her up, marveling at the sway of her hips. When they were almost at the top, she stopped and said, "I want you to look at the water pressure vent. It's corroded almost through."

His gaze followed her fingers and, sure enough, the vent was in terrible condition. "How long has this been here?"

"Since I was a kid."

"I get that you're suggesting that toxins in the water caused this corrosion. But couldn't it be age?"

She shrugged. "Perhaps, but it looks pretty terrible. I don't know what would eat away at metal like that except something caustic. I don't think it's your garden-variety rust."

"But you don't know that. Look, I'll take photos on my phone and add these to my file, but I'm not convinced this corrosion was created by more than natural causes. I'd have to see more proof than this to change my mind about the quality of water after seeing the latest report." He pulled out his phone and took a couple of shots of the vent. Then, phone pocketed, he eased his way down the ladder.

Back on the ground, she dusted off her black slacks. "This is the best I can do for right now, but as soon as I obtain any other proof, you'll be the first to know."

He nodded. "I'm sure I will." He looked at his watch. "It's not even been an hour. Are you certain you don't have time to show me a couple of trails? I'd be much obliged."

"I don't know. I have a one forty-five."

"That gives you plenty of time."

She sighed. "Okay. But let's get a move on. I can't be late."

He smiled inwardly. He had won the first battle, even with her resistance, and he now had every intention of winning the war.

***

The incline of the hills in no way mimicked mountain climbing, but they were steep enough to knock the breath out of Elena, making her aware that she needed to get more strenuous exercise. Her daily walks were hardly trekking.

Adam grabbed her arm from behind. She heard his labored breath before turning to see his beet-red face. "Whoa. I wasn't expecting a climb today. I only wanted you to point out the trails."

She smiled. "We're not even at the trailhead yet. Follow me." She led him slowly uphill to the markers. "I think you can take it from here, but if you go right, it will lead you to the top of this hill and onward to another. If you go left, you'll circumvent the hill and end up on a flatter trail."

He bent over, his hands on his thighs. "This is more than I'm used to in LA. I'll have to get adjusted to the altitude."

She stifled a laugh. "You're a real city slicker, aren't you?" Of course, she didn't let on how challenging the trek had been for her too.

He straightened. "Not for long. That's why I wanted to get out here. I need to build up my respiratory muscles."

"You mean your lungs."

"Yeah, those."

She checked her watch. "Oops, I better head back. Gotta keep that teacher appointment, then I'm off to the office."

He looked a bit deflated. Or was it exhausted? "Do you really have to go so soon? I'd love to have someone to explore this park with."

"Wish I could, but I do have appointments. Some other time."

He smiled at her, but his eyes held a solemn expression. It made her wonder what was eating at him.

"I'd like that. It's tough being a stranger in a new place. I don't know anyone except the executives at the power company, and we're not exactly on pal-around terms."

Even if he was a representative of the devil, he was a human being with feelings. Occupational hazard this empathy, but she sensed his loneliness. "I don't usually do this so soon after meeting someone, but my folks have a Sunday dinner every week. It's rather informal, but people often stop by and grab a bite. I'm sure they'd be happy to have you and it might make you feel more at home here."

His eyes lit up. "Yeah, I'd like that. I might have to go into LA this weekend to take care of some business, but if I don't, I'll plan on stopping by." He entered her parents' address into his phone. "Is there a way to contact you to let you know?"

Surprised by her impulsive behavior and relieved he might not make it, she said, "You don't have to call. Show up any Sunday. It's always an open house at the Marquez place."

"Thank you. You don't know how much this means to me. I appreciate all your help."

Another glance at her watch told her she couldn't linger. "Gotta go." And she was off, getting down the hill as quickly as possible.

Chapter 4

In the cramped kitchen of the Marquez home, Elena moved plates aside, placed two pots in a cabinet, and piled old newspapers outside the back door, then she poured herself another cup of coffee. She carried the cup out to the flagstone patio her dad had recently installed at her mother's request. Her mother loved to sit outside, but her fair skin burned in the relentless California sunshine. Dad had added a patio cover and sheets of fiberglass overhead. The patio had become her mother's sanctuary and the new setting for Sunday night family get-togethers.

Elena watched her step so she didn't spill the hot liquid, but the sound of Adam's voice made her raise her eyes and she dribbled coffee onto the flagstone. Too distracted to care, she spotted him standing next to the round white plastic table chatting with her mother and father.

She tensed in anticipation and wariness. She'd never actually expected him to show up for dinner even after he'd been invited, which led her to question why she'd invited him in the first place. Clearly, the social worker in her wanted to take care of the wounded child in everyone. That need had led her to her ex, Ron, and all the years of unhappiness she'd endured trying to save him.

While Adam might be a little lonely, she couldn't figure out why he wanted to be here. She didn't trust his motivation knowing how eager he was to persuade her to accept the utility's agenda. Was his appearance part of a plan to convince her of the company's sincerity? She would have to find a way to politely but clearly let him know his ploy wouldn't work.

"Elena, look who came by. Your friend, Adam." Her dad laughed heartily as though in on a cosmic joke. Her parents were always alert for an available man who might be the one who would marry their daughter and help give them more grandchildren.

A sheepish smile lit up Adam's rugged face. "Good to see you, Elena."

She didn't quite know what to say since she couldn't exactly second the sentiment, so she continued in silence to the table. She set her coffee cup down where she had been seated. "I'm surprised you're not in LA." Her voice carried enough of a bite that her mother looked up.

"I came back early. I didn't want to miss your kind dinner invitation."

Or an opportunity to wheedle his way into her life and charm her off-course in her potential collision with the power company. For a tense moment, she locked eyes with him.

Her mother pointed to an empty chair. "Have a seat, Adam. We're thrilled you were able to make it. I'll get you a cup of coffee and a plate of enchiladas."

Adam looked relieved. "Thanks. I'm famished after the long drive."

Out of the corner of her eye, Elena noticed someone streaking by. She turned to see her daughter Gabriella flop down onto her grandfather's lap. "Papa, come and see the rabbits before Sal scares them off."

Elena smiled. With that old mutt, Dad had oodles of time.

"In a minute, *mi nièta*. Adam's only sat down, let me spend a moment with him."

Gabriella grinned at Adam. "Hi. Want to play ping-pong?"

Great. The more she wanted to cut Adam's visit short, the more her family embraced him. Elena wagged a finger at Gabby. "Not now. Adam hasn't eaten yet. You can ask him after dinner."

Arturo gave Gabby a playful squeeze on her arm and she let out a squeal of delight.

"I'll be right back." She sprang off his lap and rushed from the patio.

"Wait," Dad called after her, but it was too late. She had disappeared beyond the wall. "I wanted her to eat something."

"Don't worry, she'll eat when she's hungry," Elena told her dad.

"She's a cute kid," Adam said to Arturo, and without looking at Elena, he added, "like her mother."

The heat rising off Elena's cheeks could have warmed the coffee her mother had carried to the table.

"Here you are, Adam. Drink up." Mom placed the cup in front of him.

"Maybe Adam wants a beer?" Arturo picked up his can of Miller and tapped it with his free hand.

"No, thanks. I could use a coffee right now." Adam lifted the cup and took a large gulp.

Elena gave him a moment. "So how's LA?" she asked in an attempt to make small talk before she sent him packing. She caught him with a mouthful of beans and enjoyed watching his discomfort.

He swallowed. "It's LA. Bloated, crowded, polluted, but also busy, exciting. Nothing's changed since I moved here."

Frieda took a seat next to Elena. "Did you know Elena moved back from Los Angeles a few months ago?"

Adam looked at Elena with curiosity. "I had no idea you lived in LA. What did you do there?"

"Elena had a good job," Arturo answered for her, "with a lot of responsibility."

Elena snorted at her father's hyperbole. Sure, she had worked her way up the ranks of the department as much as you could in the few years she'd worked for the county, but her job wasn't that significant, no more than others. Even so, her father's pride touched her. "My dad exaggerates. I was a mere minion in a huge social service system."

Her mother placed a hand on Elena's arm. "You were the head of a whole unit, *mija*." She turned to Adam. "My Elena supervised other caseworkers."

"Is that so?" Adam placed his fork on his plate and held her gaze.

Clearly, she was losing ground in her quest to rid herself quickly of this lawyer, who seemed like an expert at working the house. "I supervised other workers, but my position was far from as important as my parents make it sound. Everything I do is important in their eyes."

"That's wonderful." She could swear she saw a shadow pass over his eyes, the same darkness she'd first read in him.

Her father chortled and shook his beer can at her. "Not true. You can do plenty wrong. Like the time you tried to make burritos and used sugar instead of salt. Remember that *vieja*?"

Mom joined in his laughter. "And the time she let the skunk into the house because it looked like a cat." They both howled until tears welled in her mother's eyes and rolled down her chubby cheeks.

Elena didn't know whether to crawl under the table and hide or join them in their merriment at her expense. "There goes my fan club."

She looked at Adam and noticed the gleam in his eyes. She tried to see her family through his perspective, and smiled. They were wonderful, and they loved her. She couldn't help but wonder what his family was like. "Thanks for keeping me humble."

When the laughter finally died, Adam asked, "So how long do you intend to stay in Vandasillo?"

Frieda grasped the table's edge. "A long time, if I have any say in it."

Elena patted her mother's whitened knuckles. "I have no plans to leave any time soon."

Gabby raced across the flagstones and into the table, knocking over a glass of water.

"Careful, *niña*." Mom stood up. "I'd better find a towel before that ends up in someone's lap."

Totally oblivious to the damage, Gabriella pulled on her grandfather's sleeve. "Come on, *Abuelo*. You promised."

Dad rose slowly. "Okay. Okay. I'm coming." He hobbled off after Gabby with Sal bringing up the rear.

Elena watched the tiny procession while she stemmed the flow of liquid with a paper napkin. Mom joined in cleaning the table and soon the napkin and towel were drenched. "I'll get another towel."

Elena took off for the kitchen and searched through drawers until she came upon a clean, dry towel, hoping that by the time she returned, Adam would be taking his leave. Instead, when she reached the patio, her dad had rejoined the group, and with Gabby on his lap, he was joking with Adam.

Half-hidden by the doorframe, Elena watched the easy interaction between her family and Adam Slater. They spoke with him as though they had known him forever, as though he had always been a part of their lives and always would be. She resented the way he manipulated their openness and good nature.

Especially after Ron.

Although her parents had never said an unkind word against Ron, they were always guarded in his presence. They never quite trusted him. For simple farmers, they were pretty astute where other people were concerned. On the other hand, she couldn't help thinking if her family took such a liking to Adam so quickly, perhaps he was truly someone likable, someone she could trust.

Or, as she suspected, he was one of the smoothest and most convincing con-men she had ever met.

***

Elena's father moved behind her mother's seat and placed a hand under her elbow. "It's past our bedtime." He helped her to her feet. We ought to leave the youngsters alone." He winked at Elena.

Her mom glanced anxiously over at her. "Do you need anything else?"

The thought of being left alone with Adam made Elena uncomfortable. She had better ensure his departure with her own. She stood and reached for her mother's plate, but Mom jerked the plate away from her hand. "Sit. I can take care of that."

"But Mom—"

Frieda placed a finger over her lips. "Shh. I don't want a fight. Now is there anything else you need?"

"You've been more than gracious," Adam said.

"Then goodnight." Her mother hoisted the plate and hobbled after her husband into the darkened house.

Elena stretched and yawned. A perfect opportunity to help him on his way. "I'm spent. Aren't you tired?"

"Not yet." Adam swallowed the shortbread cookie he was eating with his coffee. "Your family is great. You're so lucky."

She took a sip of coffee, aware of her mixed emotions. On the one hand, she had been dying all evening to rid herself of him, and on the other, a bewildering, almost magnetic force made her want to prolong the agony and keep him close.

Had her parents' easy manner with him played a role in her ambivalence? And did her ambivalence play a part in his reluctance to leave?

"I know. I count my blessings every day, especially now, when I don't know what I'd do without their support." She took another sip of coffee. "My folks are so obvious though."

A small smile creased his lips. "They're wonderful people even if they're lousy matchmakers."

An unexpected pain pierced her chest. "They like you."

Adam thoughtfully bit off a piece of cookie and chewed. "I guess I should have told them I'm engaged to be married."

The pain deepened. Engaged? Why hadn't he mentioned that to her earlier? But why should he? Their relationship was purely business. Now her desire to see him leave was even more acute. Before she said or did something that expressed her disappointment, she took a sip of coffee. "Don't worry, I'll have a talk with them in the morning."

"What will you tell them?"

"That you're a lawyer for the power company and not a potential suitor." There, she had drawn a line in the sand. "You have to understand their motives are pure. They simply want to see me happy so they clutch at every straw."

He sat stone still in the half-light of the citron candle, watching her through partially shaded eyes that revealed nothing of what he might be thinking. "How do you think they'll react?"

"They'll probably feel a little foolish, but they'll recover."

He placed elbows on the table and leaned forward. "No, I mean, will I still be welcome in your home?"

Why was he so intent on being with her family? "I can't see why not. My parents are always happy to have company."

He sat back. "I'm so new around here, you and your family are the only people I really know. I'd hate to be banished."

She laughed but felt no humor. It annoyed her that he would only need her as a part-time fill-in for his LA friends. "I'm sure you'll always be welcome here."

"And how about you? Will I always be welcome with you?"

She stopped her cup in mid-air and placed it back in its saucer. "I can be friendly, Adam, but I can't be your friend. It would be a conflict of interest."

Silence. Cicadas filled the quiet with their incessant humming. The smell of fertile soil and blooming jasmine wafted through the air. She lifted a ladyfinger off the plate and allowed the sweet delicate dough to melt on her tongue.

"I understand what you're saying, but we're both mature and intelligent. We certainly wouldn't let friendship interfere with our work." He wiped his mouth with a napkin and folded it in two. "I'd still like you to show me around a few more of the local trails."

She wasn't certain why he'd force the issue. It would be dangerous territory for her to travel, but she couldn't entirely suppress the urge to explore it. "I'd only consider it if you promise you won't discuss work when we're off duty. I won't listen to any persuasion or argument in favor of the power plant's position after hours. And I'll certainly never allow any feelings for you to influence my stand." Even as she spoke she wondered if she could use this opportunity to turn the tables, to sway him to her way of thinking. Two could play this game.

***

Adam watched Elena in the flickering candlelight. He loved how it danced across her high cheekbones, lit her dark eyes. He appreciated her willingness to give him a chance. "I know that," he said, although he didn't totally believe it. If he could only maneuver a foot in the crack and slowly enlarge it, he would be in a position to shine a light on the power plant's argument. Elena was an emotional woman. All he had to do was gain her trust and she would become his ally in the community rather than his adversary. "I've been terribly lonely here. I'd appreciate the company."

"I'll think about it, but I'm still not sure it's a good idea."

He shrugged. "Would it be okay if I mention work now?"

"What is it?"

"One of the reasons I stopped by was to tell you something I forgot to mention earlier. I've tentatively scheduled a time for you to visit the power plant. Rhoades has offered to show you the sights."

Her eyes opened wider. "That's an offer I couldn't refuse. Let me know when and I'll be there."

"Wednesday at one. And Elena"—he sent her a small smile— "I'd still like to take a hike even though I have a feeling you've been wanting me to take a hike all evening."

"Guilty as charged." She laughed. "I'll think about your request."

A breeze caused the candle to flicker and the light to dance across her face. He could see the depth of her intelligent eyes, the cleft in her chin illuminated by the glow. Here was a woman he truly admired—a woman of conscience, a woman of strength.

Even though he had a goal to convert her to his way of thinking, he vowed at that moment that whatever happened, he would never do anything to harm her or her family.

Chapter 5

"Where does the water go?" Elena yelled at the top of her lungs to be heard over the deafening cacophony of the power plant machinery, the noise so great it sounded as though she had stuck her ear against a gunned car engine and could hear nothing else. Despite the earplugs she wore, the sound never abated. She cringed for the men and women who worked the plant.

Harold Rhoades stood by her side and pointed up to a large drum, about twenty feet across, far above their heads. "In there."

She looked past Adam, a few steps ahead of her, at the huge gunmetal-gray, three-story building, basically a shell except for the immense machinery surrounding her. Everywhere she saw color-coded tubing running in and out of equipment and instruments of all sizes and shapes. The crashing pistons pounding and generators grinding filled her head, making it throb.

Adam had slowed down and now strode by her side. He took her elbow and steered her behind Rhoades toward a room labeled "Laboratory" on the door. Inside, a woman in a white jacket placed test tubes in an oscillator and turned it on. The vibration added to the multitude of sounds.

When Rhoades closed the door behind them, it cut down on the noise. Elena released a breath of relief and rubbed her aching ears. "That makes heavy metal music sound as quiet as a tomb. How can anyone stand it in there for long?"

Rhoades offered her a weak smile. With his bland gray suit, thinning dishwater brown hair and pallid skin, he could have been any man and not the chief executive of a major power company. She had expected more flash from her main opponent and felt a small, surprising sense of disappointment.

"They adjust to it especially well since they're generously compensated by the company."

Elena removed her earplugs, too. *Isn't everything in life a trade-off?* But she wasn't convinced she could tolerate the plant for any price.

Rhoades gestured to the woman in white. "This is one of our scientists, Dr. Barbara Zantz. Dr. Zantz is testing wastewater from our cooling towers right now to ensure it meets the EPA standards for safety. We have the newest and most advanced equipment on the market to test our water and make certain it's well above minimum standards before it is discharged into leach fields. We treat all our water before we dispose of it." He turned to Dr. Zantz. "Can I have a small glass of that water?"

"Of course." She poured water from a vial into a paper cup and handed it to him.

Rhoades drank the water and wiped his lips with fingertips. "As you can see, the water coming out of the plant is safe enough to drink."

"What about the smoke rising off the two towers?" Elena asked.

Rhoades exchanged a grin with Zantz. "That isn't smoke, Ms. Marquez, it's steam. Those are cooling towers where heat is absorbed by the water which turns it into water vapor."

"So are you saying there's nothing toxic in the water?" Adam asked, looking like he believed every word Rhoades uttered.

"I haven't said that at all. Let's move into the control room and let Dr. Zantz do her work. We'll pick up in there." Rhoades led them into a large room full of panels with gauges and alarms. One of the alarms sounded and intermittently flashed a red light.

A large man in Levis and plaid shirt hit a switch. "That high temp bearing alarm is showing on the number two feed pump. Go down and check it, will you, Joe?"

A skinny man with slicked-back blond hair said, "Okay," opened the door to leave, and the room was filled with the roar of the plant.

After the automatic door closed and they could hear themselves think, Rhoades led them past a large panel of switches and dials. "This is our control room. It's the nerve center of the operation. Everything is monitored from here."

He directed them into a back office where he gestured toward two padded leather armchairs behind a large modern maple desk. While Adam and Elena took seats, Rhoades seated himself in a high-back swivel chair on the opposite side of the desk. "You asked about the toxicity of the water. Is that right?" He pushed the wire rims up on his nose and waited until Adam nodded. "Actually, we add chemicals to the water before we heat it to protect the equipment, but it's at negligible levels and could not be responsible for any medical problems downstream."

Rhoades sounded so sincere and honest, and Adam looked so convinced, yet Elena wondered if this was all an act. She sat forward. "What happens with the treated water?"

"The water has been treated with detoxifiers. It's chlorinated. Before it's discharged from the plant, it has to be declared safe."

"Where does it go when you dispose of it?" Adam asked.

"Haven't you seen the pond and leach fields out back?" Rhoades indicated the rear of the building with a swipe of the hand.

"Never," Adam said.

"Well, then it's time to take you on a trip." Rhoades rose and led them back through the plant and out a rear service door. Not far from the building's rear wall, pipes ran into a pond. Bright green algae tinged the edge of the pond and the fields beyond.

Rhoades held out his hand, palm up. "This is where the water I drank came from. As you can see it's clearer than the water in a city reservoir, helped along by our treatments and the algae that absorbs and breaks down impurities. I don't think you can find any better water anywhere in our industrialized society." He turned to Elena. "I do believe, Ms. Marquez, I wouldn't mind having this water come out of my faucets."

Elena looked over at Adam, who looked back with a faint smile of triumph in his eyes. He obviously was sold on what Rhoades said. Perhaps he was right, and she was pursuing the wrong source, but she had to find out for herself.

***

"This is terrible." Maria Ortega cupped her chin in both hands and rolled her head from side to side.

Maria had arrived at Elena's office for her food stamps armed with the bad news of the day. "My good friend Selena saw the doctor in Fresno yesterday. She has the blood cancer." Maria rocked in her seat. "She came by last night to tell me."

"What made her see the doctor?" Elena asked.

"She was weak. Tired. Couldn't work a full day." Maria stopped rocking and looked Elena directly in the eye. "The doctor told her she might not have much longer. What will become of her *niños*?"

Elena put aside the stamps. "You're in no condition to worry. It's my job to help her out."

Tears formed at the corners of Maria's chocolate brown eyes. "But the baby, Elena. Will something bad happen to my baby?"

Elena wanted to reassure the distraught woman, but what could she say? With the closest doctor in Fresno, she'd have similar concerns. A nurse practitioner visited Vandasillo once a week, but without personnel and the proper facility, the nurse was ill prepared to deal with the complications of pregnancy. "Have you asked the doctor about an amniocentesis or an ultrasound?"

Maria leaned forward so that her belly touched the wooden desk. "An ultra what?"

"It's a device that takes a video of the baby. Shows a picture. You can even see if it's a boy or a girl."

Maria made a grunting sound. "Every time I ask that nurse for something, she pats me on the hand and tells me I worry for nothing. I am not a worrier, Elena. You know that."

Elena knew nothing of the sort. Every time Maria appeared she brought with her accounts of death and disaster. Funny how people fooled themselves when their behavior was so obvious to others. "Do you want me to call the doctor in Fresno and tell him what's been going on in Vandasillo? Perhaps he doesn't know. I'll explain the health crisis and ask him to test you."

"*Muchas gracias*, Elena. I know he will listen to you."

No one else took her concerns seriously, not even Adam Slater, so why would a doctor believe her? Still, she had to try to alert him. If she could convince him of the problem, he'd make a terrific ally. "I'll do what I can, but I can't promise results. We'll see what happens."

Maria laid a hand on her abdomen. "I want him—Pablo thinks it's a boy because I am *grande*—to be healthy. That is all I ask of God."

"I want your baby to be healthy, too." Elena smiled her most uplifting smile. "And wealthy and wise wouldn't hurt."

Maria smiled in return, but the sadness and fear still lingered in her eyes. "I hope he is born with all his fingers and toes." Slowly, she maneuvered herself out of the chair, using her hands to push her bloated vessel of a body to standing. "Leave a message after you talk to the doctor."

"I promise." Elena walked around the desk and laid a hand on Maria's shoulder. "In the meantime, you take care of yourself and your *niño*."

"*Adios*." The screen door slammed behind Maria as she left.

Elena took a seat by the scratched walnut desk and dialed Adam's LA number. His secretary answered.

"Adam Slater's office. May I help you?"

"Is Adam available?"

"I'm afraid he's in a meeting," his secretary said. "Can I take a message?"

"Will you tell him to call Elena Marquez when he's done? I need to speak to him."

***

Harold Rhoades rolled a ballpoint pen between thumb and fingers and stared at the wall behind Adam's head. "I understand this is more complicated than you originally thought, but that's not the plant's problem. We're doing our part to police ourselves. We've done more than most power plants. Check around. Our policy of paying for a quarterly water and soils report is almost unheard of."

Adam knew he had to temper his response. "I'm not accusing the plant of any wrongdoing, but there's a virulent problem in this community. Perhaps the plant could take the initiative in trying to assess the source of the problem? That would help to place the guilt where it belongs and improve the plant's image." Adam tapped the report in his hand. "This is helpful, but you could be doing more."

Rhoades looked down at his manicured fingernails. "We could always do more, Adam, but we only have limited resources." He pointed one of his fingers at the file. "Why should we take on anything else when it's obvious from that report we are not to blame for any environmental problems?"

"Think of it as a public relations pitch. From what I understand you're not too popular in the community since you imported most of your workers. It's natural you might take the rap when a problem arises. Why not show the residents that you're concerned enough to help out?"

Rhoades made a hissing noise through the gap in his front teeth. "This isn't a popularity contest we're running here. This is a business. A business that brings light and heat to homes all around the county. We do what we can to make life better for these people. I don't believe we have to do anything else."

Adam looked into Rhoades's watery, empty eyes and swallowed down the frustration that lodged itself in his throat. No use trying to convince Rhoades to do anything differently. Clearly, he felt justified in his position. "Okay. So, all you want me to do is show the latest report to the social worker. What good will that do?"

"Proves that we're in the right." Rhoades went back to fidgeting with the pen. "Can't question statistics. All the numbers are the same as before."

"All right, but it doesn't seem to be making much of an impression on Ms. Marquez. She doesn't seem too awestruck with your numbers."

Rhoades stopped his activity. "It's your job to convince Ms. Marquez of our innocence. That's why we're paying your firm big bucks. If you're not able to handle this—"

Adam raised a hand. "I'll do my best." He had too much to lose here to allow Rhoades to replace him. His future rested on this job. He stood and walked to the door. "I'll let you know how it goes."

When he turned to look back, Rhoades caught his eye. "I expect results, Adam. Do you understand?"

Adam nodded and left the room uncertain he could produce what Rhoades expected. Uncertain he wanted to.

Chapter 6

A malnourished-looking waitress at El Rancho restaurant with spiked fire-engine-red hair placed a plate of *enchiladas*, rice and beans in front of Adam and an order of *chile rellenos* before Elena. Elena took a bite of the dish: a rich blend of battered chile stuffed with cheese and covered with a delicious hot sauce. She chewed, swallowed, then put her fork on the plate and looked up at Adam, who was lifting his fork. "I have bad news."

Adam lowered the fork. "What?"

"Two new cases of leukemia have been diagnosed locally."

"Damn." He sat for a moment, eyes lowered. "I'm sorry to hear that."

"So are the families." She laid a hand on the table by Adam's arm. With his sleeve rolled up, she could see his sinewy strength. "It's statistically impossible for this one community to be so hard hit by this cancer. Something's at the root of this."

He leaned back, his food untouched, and stared at her.

She had his attention, now all she needed was his help. "I've had a little chance to get to know you, and I believe you're a good and honorable person." She leaned toward him. "Even though you represent the power plant, you wouldn't condone harming innocents. We both want what's in the best interest of others."

He cocked his head to the side and narrowed his eyes. "And your point is?"

"That we work together. We can help one another uncover the truth."

He reached into the briefcase by his side and extracted a file that he handed to her. "I'd be glad to work with you, but the latest power plant report confirms their earlier results. If you're convinced the power company is behind these problems, I don't know how I can help you."

Elena looked through the report. As he said, the figures were almost identical to the original ones. "So how do you explain the rash of cancer?"

The waitress stopped by their table and pointed at Adam's plate. "Anything wrong?"

"No, it's fine," he replied. "Thank you."

"Want anything else?" she asked.

Elena shook her head and the waitress turned to serve another table.

Adam watched as she stepped away. "Good waitress."

A kid behind Elena kicked the seat and squealed with delight. She moved aside. "So what's your analysis?"

"Oh yeah." He gave her a sheepish grin. An adorable boyish grin. A grin that could melt hearts, but she'd never allow it. She braced herself.

"As I said earlier, the people in the fields are exposed to all sorts of chemicals. Any one of them could be the culprit. You're fixated on the power plant, but—"

"You make me sound like a nut case or a conspiracy theorist. I'm not totally inflexible. I'm suspicious, and with good reason. Farmers in other communities use the same chemicals that are applied in Vandasillo, but they aren't having the same problems." She wiped her mouth with a napkin. "The farmworkers have noticed a growing change since the power plant was built. Even though many of them don't speak the language, they're acutely aware that something serious is going on."

"But they might be overreacting. Frightened. Overwhelmed. Naturally, they'd want to point fingers. When anyone feels out of control over anything, they tend to want to place blame. Makes them feel better." He took a bite of an enchilada. "Mmm mmm, good."

"But what if they're right?"

"Remember learning about the Salem witch trials and the McCarthy commission? People make mistakes out of fear."

Hardly an apt comparison. As Adam ate his meal with gusto, Elena strategized. How could she convince him to work with her? The last thing she wanted was to work against him. It didn't help her cause.

"Tell you what. I have a plan. What if we both do our homework and see what we can come up with? I'll study the water and run an independent analysis, and you look into the fertilizers and pesticides. Then we can compare notes."

"You're wasting your money, Elena. The plant's already done the research."

"Anything else you want here?" the waitress asked. She stood by the table, pad in hand.

"The check, please," Adam told her.

The waitress tore the bill off the pad and handed it to Adam. He looked it over.

"You wouldn't accept that check without studying it. Wasn't it you who said," Elena lowered her voice to mimic his, "'people make mistakes.'"

He shrugged.

"Then why should I accept these reports at face value?"

"Because the results have been substantiated more than once."

"But consider the source."

He put down his cup with an abrupt clank. "Are you accusing the power plant of fraud?" Anger tinged his voice. She didn't want to alienate him. She wanted him to see things from her perspective. "Of course not, but there's strong potential for bias. I thought an independent analysis of the groundwater might be in order here. I'm willing to pay for it and let the chips fall where they may. This will get me off your back once and for all. If I'm wrong, I won't bother you anymore."

A twinkle lit his eyes. "You never bother me. I actually look forward to our little confrontations. It's good for practice. After you, facing a Senate investigating committee would be a piece of cake."

She laughed but her gaze remained glued to his.

Adam held her gaze and she could feel the flush spread across her cheeks. What could she be thinking? Wasn't he basically a taken man?

"Okay, I'll find out what I can." He withdrew his wallet and placed two twenties on the table. When she went for her purse, he stopped her hand with his. "It's on me."

"No."

"Yes. You can treat another time."

"Thanks, but don't forget the next one's on me."

He paid the bill and walked her to her car. By the driver's door, she turned to him. In the sunlight, the crown of his reddish-brown hair lit like a halo, his eyes sparkled. They stood so close she could feel the heat rise off his skin, smell the manly scent of aftershave wafting toward her.

He glanced at his watch. "I'm late for an appointment. Have to run. Don't forget to do your assignment. You'll be graded on it next week."

He turned on his heels and marched toward his car, leaving her a bit breathless and confused.

***

At the end of a long morning of catching up on paperwork and filing reports, Elena's least favorite job-related activities, she gathered up her purse and briefcase to leave for lunch. When she opened the office door, which had been closed against any and all distractions, she ran smack into Maria Ortega. "Oh."

"Sorry." Maria's normally full face was lined with worry, her eyes beady and intense. "I have to talk to you." She patted down her disheveled thrift-store-quality mint green dress. "Are you going out?"

Elena gestured toward her desk. "Must be important. Come on in." She trailed Maria to the padded side chair, waited for her to shift her weight into the seat and leaned against the desk.

"You must visit Lorena," Maria said, facial lines deepening.

"Why? What's going on? I saw her a couple of days ago."

"Yolanda told me she refuses to eat. She only sits and stares at the ceiling. Please, Elena, she needs your help."

Elena pushed herself upright. "Sounds serious. I'll drop by on my way home for lunch."

"And, Elena—" Maria bit her lip. "While you're at the camp, look in on Teresa Salinas. She gave birth to a child with a bad arm and leg." Maria clutched her stomach. "I do not like to hear that."

"Did you see the doctor about that ultrasound I recommended?"

"Not yet. Did you talk to the doctor like you said?"

She had, and he had sounded arrogant and inconclusive. While he hadn't said it to her out loud, she gathered he wouldn't take her suggestion seriously. She hoped he was more responsive toward his patients, although she doubted it. "Yes, but he wanted to speak to you about the pregnancy before making any decisions. Give him a holler. Okay?"

Maria squirmed to standing. "I will." At the office door, she turned to Elena. "And you will see Lorena?"

"I'm on my way now."

Maria sighed and pushed through the screen door.

***

Lorena stared past Elena, a blank look in her eyes. "I no hungry."

Elena shifted to make herself comfortable on the narrow, wooden bench. "But you have to eat. You can't starve yourself. You'll die."

A single tear trickled down Lorena's face and cut a pale channel in the dust on her cheek. Her hair hadn't been combed and lay about her face in wisps and clumps. She wore the same ratty t-shirt and baggy black knit pants she'd had on two days earlier.

The untouched shack looked dingy. Even though surrounded by other plywood and tarp-covered *temporary housing*, it stood out because the others were immaculately maintained. Suspended in the sunlight streaming in through the uncovered doorway, dust coated the few battered pieces of furniture.

Lorena absently wiped the tear from her face and smeared dirt across her cheek. "For what do I live, Elena? My life, it is over."

Elena's heart hurt hearing this resignation from someone so young. Most people in the migrant community were resilient. They had weathered so many storms, they had learned to pick up the pieces after the damage was done, sweep up the mess and go on. But Lorena was different. She didn't have the emotional strength of others.

"You have a lot to live for. You're young. I know this has been hard for you, but you have your family. You can pull your life back together, have another child. You have to stay strong. If not for yourself, for your mother and father and all your sisters."

Lorena pressed her head into her hands, her shoulders shaking with violent sobs. Elena wrapped an arm around her and held her through a torrent of tears.

When Lorena lifted her head, tears wet her face and the front of her dress was stained a forest green. "I am sorry, Elena."

Elena squeezed her. "You have nothing to be sorry about. I'm glad you trust me enough to let me see your pain. It means a great deal to me."

Lorena threw her arms around Elena's neck. "*Muchas gracias*. I need to remind me of my family in Mexico. They need me to send money or they will no have enough to feed all the little ones." She hugged Elena and then let go. "You are my saint, Elena, sent here by God."

Elena straightened her coral-colored blouse. "Or at least by County Social Services."

For the first time, Lorena gave her a half-hearted smile.

"Now I want you to eat something. I'm on my way home for lunch. My mother has cooked up a batch of her signature tamales. I'm going to return in an hour with a plate."

Lorena pressed a palm to her abdomen. "I no can eat."

"Wait until you taste my mother's tamales before you say that." She fluttered her fingers at Lorena as she hurried out the door, stopping in front of Teresa Salinas's shack. She poked her head in the open doorway, taking a second to adjust to the dim light. Three ghostly figures inside rushed toward her.

Heriberto approached first. He squinted into the bright sunlight. "Who's there?"

"It's me, Elena. I've come to see Teresa and the baby."

Teresa poked her head out around him. "Elena? Elena Marquez. Come in."

Elena stepped over a slinky and a pile of Lincoln Logs as she entered the room. Teresa and Heriberto had three children, ranging in age from two to seven. Now they had a fourth mouth to feed, a child with developmental disabilities to boot. How would they be able to cope with all this?

She sidestepped an open coloring book, trying to avoid crushing crayons into a piece of industrial-grade carpet. The Salinases had lived in the camp for a couple of years and managed to decorate their plywood lean-to with carpet remnants and odds and ends. A piece of sectional served as a couch against one wall. Two wobbly chairs sat before an ancient Formica-covered, particleboard Parsons table at the opposite side of the room. The room was sparse, but except for the children's playthings, spotless, and not unpleasant. She barely missed tripping over a ladder truck left by one of the boys. "How's the new baby?"

Teresa took her by the arm over to a bassinet.

"He's beautiful, Elena, except for this." Teresa pulled a gray wool blanket off the baby to reveal one of the most adorable infants she'd ever seen. His huge brown eyes watched her every move and dimples played on both cheeks when he smiled. All she could see when she glanced down was a perfectly formed child until she spied the stunted arm and leg on his left side. She squelched the shock that spread through her.

"He's a gorgeous baby." Elena reached down and allowed him to encircle her finger with his right hand. "And he has a firm grip."

"But his left arm and leg are no right," Heriberto said. "He is no like the other children. The doctor says he need special care. How we pay for it?"

"That's why I stopped by. I want you to know I will do everything I can to help you with this. There are programs that help children with special needs like... What did you name him?"

"Carlos," Teresa said.

"I'll make the necessary arrangements, but I'll need your cooperation."

"*No problema*, Elena. We do what you say."

Chapter 7

Elena glanced at the clock in her Tercel. *Damn*. She had worked through lunch again. She hated to always stick her mother with Gabriella, but she had no choice. Some days were too chock full.

As soon as she arrived at her office, she called Mom and explained herself. Of course, she was as loving and gracious as always, but that didn't appease Elena's guilt. She wished she could be more available to Gabby even though she knew her mother was a terrific substitute. She found it hard to balance her career with childrearing: it'd become a high-wire-while-juggling-plates act if she ever saw one, especially since the problems with the power plant.

With only a few minutes remaining before her next appointment, she pulled a packet of trail mix from her desk drawer. While she crunched, she dialed the 800 number she had downloaded off the Internet for the Environmental Protection Agency. The call immediately went to a mechanical voice that directed her to push the button keyed to the hotline for environmental concerns. After waiting through an all-string rendition of popular music and filling out a report, she finally heard a man's voice on the line.

"Charles Johnson, EPA. May I help you?" he asked.

"I'm Elena Marquez, a social worker in Vandasillo, California. I want to report a suspected environmental disaster."

"Could you describe the problem, Ms. Marks?"

"Marquez. Within the last year, there's been sixteen cases of leukemia diagnosed in the community and three children have been born with birth defects. This is a small farming community with a mostly migrant population. The number of new cases is exorbitant. I'm extremely suspicious and concerned."

He cleared his throat. "Has your local community health center reported this to us?"

"Not that I know of. We have only a small staff with a nurse on call and a visiting nurse practitioner. The doctor's in Fresno and rarely visits the center. I don't know how up to date and accurate their statistics are."

"Hmm." He was quiet a moment. "If you want to file a report that would be fine, but I'll have to tell you, we're quite backed up right now with a number of other hot spots. We'll follow through, but it might take a few months until we get to yours."

She doodled with a pen. "This is a serious situation. People are dying here. The ground water needs to be tested before more people die."

"We receive at least twenty tips a day from people all over the country with problems similar to yours and we only have so many on staff. We have to look into your complaint first before we proceed. Where did you get your numbers?"

She stifled a sigh of exasperation. "I'm a social worker in the community. I know what's going on."

He tapped the phone. "And you said it's a migrant community in California. Is it mainly Mexican migrants?"

Her defenses clicked into place. "Yes?"

"They might be exposed to whatever's causing the problem in Mexico. Let's be honest, Ms. Marks, the water is notoriously polluted in Mexico."

She had given up trying to correct his mispronunciation of her name. "But most of these people reside here year-round."

A tap again. "Okay. Where do you want me to send the necessary forms?"

She gave him her fax number and hung up, grateful to be done with the call. Her head throbbed from dealing with such an officious functionary who could hardly give a fig about these people's lives. She couldn't help wondering if being migrants they were more expendable to the bureaucracy in Washington than full-fledged citizens, many of whom weren't treated all that well either.

***

Later, after meeting with another client about his wife's mother, she booted up the computer and accessed the Internet, going immediately to the homepage of the Environmental Defense Fund. They were on the top of her list of environmental groups to alert to the Vandasillo predicament. She sent an email first to them first, then one to Earth Watch seeking support, direction and, if at all possible, money to undertake the necessary tests.

Her next appointment waited while she stole time to finish her emails. For now, she'd have to put her concerns aside to address the day-to-day problems of her clients, but the emerging health crisis would remain in the forefront of her mind.

***

Scanning a report in front of him, Adam leaned over his desk with his phone wedged between head and shoulder. He held the papers in front of him. "These numbers are pretty convincing, Elena. They certainly support the argument that pesticides might be at the root of the problem. The active ingredient in one product alone has caused cancers and birth defects where it's been used extensively. Look what's happening with the United States program of defoliation in Colombia. There are rampant medical problems wherever the government has sprayed."

"I'm sure you're right about the pesticides, but I've done my own investigation. They've been using the exact same pesticides on these fields since nineteen seventy-one. The recent rash of problems didn't begin until nineteen ninety-nine. Explain that." Her voice sounded soft but sincere.

He sat back, scratched his head. Hell if he knew, but he wasn't about to back out of the argument. That would be un-lawyerly. "Maybe the damage is cumulative and takes years to manifest."

"I'd believe that if a number of these families hadn't arrived in the last two or three years. Those puzzle pieces don't fit together."

She made a sound that he could easily mistake for resignation, but he knew it to be determination. She was at least as stubborn as he, if not more. Still, he couldn't help admiring her tenacity. Her willingness to pursue what she believed continued to astonish him.

"The only element that has altered in the community," she continued, "is the introduction of the power plant in ninety-five. Nothing else has changed."

"Tell you what," he said. "We're not going to resolve this over the phone. How about if I fax you the pesticide report and you take a gander at it. I'll be in Los Angeles. When I return, let's sit down and hash this out further."

***

Elena knew what he meant. He would be spending time with his fiancée and the thought instantly provoked irritation. Despite efforts to ignore her ridiculous reaction, the catch in her voice was undeniable. "How long will you be gone?" *Damn*. She wished she hadn't sounded like such a clingy woman.

"Only for two days. I'll be back by Monday. Let's set a time to meet now."

Any time would work for Elena. She hated that she wanted to see his bright, brown eyes and his warm, wide smile. As much as she'd like to deny it, she had grown attached to him. Under the circumstances, that thought made her squirm. She glanced at her schedule book. "I'm free between two-thirty and three."

"Schedule me in."

Elena hung up, closed her office door and lowered herself into the gray cloth swivel chair, staring out the window. Why did she feel so uncomfortable about Adam's situation? He was only a friend and a distant one at that. She swiped at her dress, mentally brushing away her earlier feelings. She had to maintain her objectivity around Adam, or she would not be doing the responsible thing. And she prided herself on being responsible.

***

Adam took Brittany by the arm and led her to his Jeep. Once in his seat, he clicked on his seatbelt. "How about lunch at Chez Henri and a walk around Santa Monica?"

She played with her hair in the visor mirror. "I promised Dan and Kate we'd meet them on Melrose. They're waiting for us."

He turned to her, but she kept her eyes glued on her image in the mirror. "But we haven't spent a moment alone together since I returned to town. I want time with you before I go back to Vandasillo."

She flipped the visor up. "Don't be silly. We've been together morning, noon and night since Friday. How much time do you need?"

"It's not time, Brit. It's time alone. We're always with your friends."

She raised her perfectly arched brows. "What would we do alone?"

"How about talk?"

"We can talk in the car on the way to Melrose."

"I don't mean chatter. I mean talk like two people in love who are about to be married. Talk about things that really matter to us."

Her eyes widened. "But I do talk about what matters to me."

That's what he was afraid of. Nothing else seemed to matter to Brittany than her friends and the rhythm of her social life. She might be one of the most strikingly beautiful women he'd ever laid eyes on, but he needed more than a trophy wife. "Maybe you could call Kate and cancel. Just this once."

"It's too late for that. They're waiting for us."

When he frowned, she reached out a hand. "How about if I set time aside for the two of us the next time you're in town?" She batted dark eyelashes at him. "Promise."

What could he say if she already had the day planned? "All right," he said with resignation, then started the engine and took the 101 south to LA. At a light on Fountain Street, a toothless woman stood by the side of the road, speaking loudly to herself. Her ragged clothes and unkempt hair heralded her condition.

Brittany shook her lovely head. "Why do they permit people like that to roam the streets?"

"It's too bad the authorities can't figure out a way to treat schizophrenia and help the mentally ill. Their living situations are deplorable," he agreed.

She grunted her disdain. "I wish they'd round them up and get them out of sight. They're so nasty and dirty. They really bum me out."

He stared at her. "How do you think they feel?"

"Oh, Adam." She laughed. "Do you really think they're that aware? Look at her."

The light turned green and Adam hit the accelerator. No use discussing social issues with Brittany. They'd never see eye-to-eye. He thought of Elena and imagined her in a debate with Brittany. It would be interesting to see her try to hold her own against someone with a real conscience and concern for others.

He turned down Melrose and surprised himself by finding a parking space close to the coffee shop where they were to meet

Brittany's friends. Dan, with his hipper-than-hip buzz cut and yin-yang tattoo, and Kate with her brow ring, waved to them from a table in the shop's rear. The glided over slate floors, past pumpkin-colored sponge-painted walls and a gold-plated espresso machine to the solid teak table and wrought iron chairs. A bleached-blonde waif of a waitress took their orders of cappuccinos and mochas.

After the beverages arrived, Brittany prattled on while Dan and Kate listened and sipped their coffees. Adam failed miserably at every attempt to tune in, much too preoccupied with the evolving controversy in Vandasillo to pay attention to her mindless chatter.

He wanted to dispel his growing discontent with their relationship, especially since she was the boss's daughter and breaking off their engagement wouldn't sit well and might cost him his job. But he couldn't shake the feeling that he was making a terrible mistake. While he hadn't been as conscious of it before, his developing respect for Elena had now made him aware that Brittany's ideas and ideals, and the essence of who she was as a person, clashed with everything he valued.

With this realization, he didn't know how much longer he could ignore his feelings.

***

The woman from the Environmental Defense Fund had placed Elena on hold so she could check out the name of a laboratory that tested water. Elena waited patiently with the phone on speaker while she made notes in a client's file.

"I have the name here," the woman said, and gave Elena all the information. "They can test a water sample and give you a rundown on the toxic substances it contains. I suggest you submit samples from two or three different places."

"How much will it cost?"

"About two or three hundred a sample, but the lab's procedures will give you a highly balanced and well-supported report."

Elena gulped. "That's a little steep on a social worker's salary."

The woman shared her agreement. "I wish we could help, but we're all tapped out after our push to pass that recent emissions standards bill. Clean air is as essential to life as clean water."

Elena nervously nibbled her pen tip. Was she working in a vacuum? "What can you do?"

"If you have verifiable evidence the water is polluted, we'd do all we can to have your case heard in Sacramento. The politicians and bureaucrats can't help but be swayed by big business. They have the deep pockets to finance campaigns that keep the old system oiled." She cleared her throat. "We can counter the politics as usual with people and pressure."

"How?" Elena asked.

"We have a network of over a million members who are willing to write to their congressperson in support of our causes. One million voters can make a difference, believe me."

Elena nodded to no one. It might take a million voters to move the power plant machinery in a more community-friendly direction. "So, if I'm able to bring you proof the water's polluted, you'll be able to help me out. Right?

"Exactly."

"Then I'll find a way to pay for the water analysis, no matter what."

The woman mumbled something inaudible to someone else. "Sorry. One of the other volunteers needed help. Now, what were you saying?"

"What happens after I generate the water report?"

"The finding will have to be linked to the power plant. That's the tough part. Regardless of what the report says, without evidence the power plant is creating the problem, our efforts will drown."

How could she verify the power plant was the source of the problem? She didn't know the answer, but if they were, she'd find a way to prove it. "At least I know where to begin. As soon as I have the initial results, I'll be back in contact."

"Please do," the woman said. "If we can do anything else, let me know. Even though this is more of a micro problem, affecting only one community, unlike the macro problems we typically undertake, we'd still be interested in helping you. The migrant workers are disenfranchised and have so little political support, we'd be available to help in any way we can."

Elena had to smile to herself. Usually, she encountered the opposite reaction. This woman's words were a breath of fresh air, or, in this case, a sip of clean water. "I'm grateful you're there."

She hung up and leaned back in her chair, hand behind head. Although she'd be hard-pressed to come up with the funds, she'd do her best. She'd already tried every source she could think of. The man at the Sierra Club had been helpful with the name of other resources, but not forthcoming with funds, and the United Farm Workers said they had their own legal department and would look into the matter. She'd have to pay out of pocket for the tests. The only unfortunate part was she'd only be able to afford a single sample. One sample was better than none and might give her enough information to see if further exploration was necessary. She hugged herself and silently prayed she had moved closer toward solving the problem.

Chapter 8

Gabriella ran toward Elena's car as she maneuvered it up the dirt driveway of the Marquez house. Elena squeezed from the seat and swung her legs to the ground, stopped by Gabby's skinny arms around her neck.

"Momma."

"Hi, sweetie." She lifted her daughter off the ground and swung her around, garnering squeals. When she lowered her to the ground, she gave her a big hug. Gabby beamed up at her and her heart swelled. What a blessing she was in Elena's life. "How about we take a walk in a bit. We haven't done that for a while."

Gabby flushed with excitement. "Now, Momma, now."

"As soon as I speak to your grandmother." She glanced up at the kitchen door, fully expecting her mother to make her usual appearance, but the doorway remained empty. She gave Gabby one last hug and looked again toward the house. No sign of Mom. "Where's Nana?"

Gabby pulled away. "On the sofa." She took Elena's hand and led her into the house.

In the living room, as Gabby had said, Mom lay on her side, quietly snoring. When Gabby rushed past Elena into the room, her mother startled awake.

"Wha..." She rubbed her eyes and looked around, confused. "You're home, *mija*. What time is it?"

"Lunchtime." Elena took a seat on the edge of her father's favorite chair, surprised to find her mother asleep in the middle of the day. "What's wrong, Mom? Don't you feel well? Do you need me to cancel my appointments and stay home this afternoon?"

Her mother righted herself to sitting, a groggy look on her face. "Of course not. This is nothing serious. A minor cold. Gabby promised to stay close to the house while I'm resting. I don't want you to disappoint your clients."

"Are you sure? You're beginning to worry me. I've seen you sick before and I can only remember one time when you had to stay in bed during the daytime."

Her mother patted her hand. "But now I'm an old woman, *mija*. I'm not a girl like you. I don't have the same strength."

Elena scrunched up her face. "Sometimes you have more energy than ten of me."

Gabby had disappeared into the kitchen and returned with Sal and a cup of coffee for her nana. She held out the steaming cup to her grandmother. "Here, Nana. This will make you feel better."

"Thank you, Gabriella. It certainly will."

Gabby handed her nana the cup, then dropped down on the sofa beside her. Sal slumped at her feet.

"I wish I had my phone right now and could snap a shot of you all together, but I know as soon I walk into the other room to find it, everything will change," Elena said. *Isn't that the way life went?*

Mom ran her hand over Gabby's hair. "She's an angel, my Gabriella."

For once Gabby sat still, and Elena was struck with how grown-up she was becoming. No longer a small child, a mysterious set of internal circumstances had been at play in her height, her shape and the planes of her face. Right before her eyes, Gabriella was changing into a lovely young woman.

Mere weeks earlier, Gabby would never have sat for so long. Elena marveled at the transition and suddenly felt old. If *she* felt old, how did her mother feel with her gangly spirited granddaughter newly emerged from her chrysalis into a long-legged butterfly?

"Please, Mom, don't be a martyr for once. If you need me, say so. None of my clients will shrivel up and blow away without my intervention today. Anyway, I promised Gabby a walk before I go back to work."

Mom sent her a grin, but her eyes failed to register any mirth. "Take your walk, but then I absolutely want you to do your job and let me do mine taking care of Gabby here." She poked Gabby in the ribs. Her granddaughter squealed, jumped up from the sofa and ran from the room, Sal slowly following. Obviously, the metamorphosis was not complete.

"You'll call if you need me?" Elena asked.

Her mother sipped her coffee. "I will."

52

"Do you want anything to eat?"

"Not right now, but there's tacos for you on the kitchen counter. Go ahead and heat them up."

She moved toward the kitchen doorway. Her mother was always so thoughtful. Elena hoped she could return the favor someday. Before she turned into the kitchen, she looked back over her shoulder. "I love you, too, Mom. I really do."

***

Later she walked hand in hand with Gabby down the dirt road and across an open field. They skipped together and Gabby led the way. Spending time with her daughter always filled Elena with joy.

"Come with me, Mama," Gabby said, grabbing her hand and leading her to a tree by the *bosque* where cottonwood trees ringed the river. "Look at this."

She followed Gabby's finger and immediately spotted a nest in one of the trees. On closer inspection, she saw the dove eggs inside. "Wow, you found a dove's nest. It looks like those eggs will hatch at any time."

Gabby was flush with excitement. "Can we come back, Mama, and see the baby birds?"

"Of course we can." She smiled down at her beautiful daughter. "We'll make a date to visit them every evening when I'm home. I wouldn't want you to miss this."

"Yeah." Gabby ran ahead of her and she had to jog to try and keep up. While her daughter ran, Elena could sense herself fill with gratitude that she could spend time with Gabby and be the parent she never felt she could fully be around Ron. It was time to heal the wounds from the hurt Ron had caused them.

***

Adam leaned back in his office chair and folded his arms over his chest. "So, how do you plan to accomplish all this? You sound like Don Quixote, flailing after windmills."

Elena took a sip of bottled water before answering. "I can do it on my own."

Adam furrowed his brow. "But you're treading old ground. Why not explore a new avenue?"

She sat forward. "All right. What's your suggestion?"

Uh-oh. Open mouth, insert foot. He had no more creative ideas than she had, but now he'd have to come up with something. "What about asking the power plant to underwrite air quality tests? Have you seen the recent report about California? It says California leads the nation in dirty air. What a distinction. Perhaps we're looking in the wrong direction."

She released a dry laugh. "Nothing against the power plant administration, but so far they don't seem intent on uncovering the truth. They seem more concerned with protecting their own interests. I'd rather see an independent study."

Of course, she might be right. "Where do you think you'll find the money for any of this?"

"The Elena Marquez fund. Where else?"

He studied her, sitting across from him, her long dark hair falling around her lovely oval face. How vulnerable she looked, with her delicate fingers intertwined in her lap. Everything about her seemed elegant and breakable, even her heart. He wanted to protect her from the pain and frustration he could see coming her way with this endeavor, but he didn't know how. He was on the other side, and what made things even more complicated, he might have to be the one to hurt her. "I don't know, Elena. I see trouble on the horizon. You're taking on an awful lot."

She smiled her Mona Lisa smile and he melted. Why did she have to be so damn appealing?

"I'm a big girl. I know what I'm doing, and I'm prepared for the consequences. All I want from you is respect for my findings."

He wished that was all he wanted from her, but with Rhoades and the firm on his back, he had to convince her she was on the wrong track. "You might think you know what's ahead, but I don't believe you have any idea. The power company has plenty of bucks to interfere with your campaign. You better be prepared for a bumpy ride."

She laughed. "What else is new? I've experienced my bumps and they never destroyed me."

"No matter what you've faced, it's probably a mere drizzle compared to the storm brewing with the company. They have the clout, the money and the backing of the state utility board. Watch out, you're playing in the major leagues now."

"I know you're trying to discourage me because you represent them, but I'm going to find out the truth. I'm in this too far to turn back. No one will discourage me, not even you." He heard the annoyance in her tone.

What could he say against such single-minded focus? "All right, Elena, but I can't help you. I thought about what you said, about our working together, but I work for them. I have an obligation to represent them unless I want to quit my job. I certainly can listen to what you say, but I'll have to weigh it with the company's best interests in mind."

"So you're saying the truth be damned. All I care about is what serves the big, fat overblown power company."

Though he desperately wanted to back her up, he had a job to do. The power company had all the data on their side. What could he say? "Whether you approve or not, I'll do my job. Right now, at least in this office, you're on the other side of the desk. I only hope that doesn't extend to outside of here."

Elena bit back the words that sprang into her head. She wanted to give him a piece of her mind for wanting to play both sides, but she could understand his conflict. They were becoming friends, weren't they? "Right now our only relationship is in this office, around this issue. All else is on hold until this issue is resolved."

"I might be your opponent in this office, but I'm your friend in the real world." His smile was meant to break down her resistance. She had to steel herself against it.

"Does that mean you'll do whatever I want once we're on the street?"

He narrowed his eyes. "And what might that be?"

She picked up on his innuendo and her face heated beneath his continued stare. "Well, actually, it's what my mother wants. She wants you to come for dinner again soon."

He snapped his fingers and said seductively, "I was hoping it was an invitation from you."

When she eyed him, he laughed. "Only teasing."

She hadn't realized her hopes were raised until after they were dashed.

She chided herself for her reaction to him.

Chapter 9

With sanitized Ball jar in hand, Elena strode down to the stream behind the power plant facility. It occurred to her that the closer she was to the plant, the stronger the link between the utility and any harmful contaminants.

Glancing around to make sure she hadn't been followed, she uncapped the jar, careful not to contaminate it. She knelt down to feel the cool air rising off the stream's surface. The gurgling water as it rushed over rocks played background music to a noisy blue jay. Not far from where she stooped on the bank, a woodpecker hammered on tree bark in pursuit of edibles. A blanket of orange and yellow poppies bloomed at her feet. This would be paradise if it weren't for the mildly metallic odor rising off the river. She wrinkled her nose against the smell.

She extended the jar over the stream and submerged it into the water. When she was certain she had gotten an adequate sample, she lifted it out.

From behind her, a baritone male voice demanded. "Wha' yuse think yuse doing?"

Stunned, she almost dropped the jar and tightened her grip on it. She glanced up and shaded her eyes with her free hand against the sun. Far above her stood a burly giant dressed in a dark blue uniform. He scowled down at her. She felt like she had as a kid, caught dousing the dog with her mother's perfumes. "Taking a water sample."

He eyed the jar she held out to him. "What for?"

The badge on the guard's lapel read, *Herman Molar, IVGE Security*. While she never lied, she thought in this situation it might be wise to modify the truth. "For my daughter's science project. She's taking water samples from around the county. Testing them for alkalinity."

"Don't yuse know yuse on private property? This land belongs to the power plant. There's signs posted around." He wagged at finger at her. "Yuse lucky I have kids. If one of the other guys caught yuse they'd turn yuse into the authorities. Beings I'm kindhearted, I'll let yuse go this once, but don't let me catch yuse here again."

With the expression on his face, she doubted he was as good-natured as he saw himself, but she wasn't in the position to quibble. The last thing she wanted to do was alert the power plant administration to her presence. "Thanks. My daughter will be grateful to you."

"Yep. Now yuse run along and don't come back."

Elena capped the jar, stuck it into her daypack and backed away. Once she was over a hill and out of the guard's sight, she broke into a sprint until she reached her car.

Back at her office, she placed the container in a box labeled for shipment to the laboratory that would test the sample. She had spoken to a woman at the lab only the day before and had followed her instructions to the letter. It would take over two weeks for the report to be returned, but then she would have a better idea of what she was facing.

She filled out the faxed form along with a check and placed them next to the jar before sealing the package. As soon as she taped the box, she ran it over to the Vandasillo post office, arriving minutes before five o'clock closing time. She handed the box to the clerk and informed him it contained breakable material. He stamped "Fragile" all over the box. That stamp was the last step in the process to ensure she received the information she needed.

The clerk dropped the box behind a curtain and called for the next in line. Now she would have to wait as patiently as possible for the test results. In the meantime, she could only hope no more disasters befell the community.

***

Much to Elena's surprise, Adam pulled up to the Marquez house mid-afternoon on Friday and caught her pruning the courtyard roses. "What are you doing here?"

He stepped from his Jeep and offered her a wide smile, one too endearing for words. She responded with a shameful, unexpected flush.

"I was on my way out of town for a couple of days and I wanted to touch base with you. I tried to call your office, but you were obviously not there. What are you doing home in the middle of the afternoon?"

"My mother hasn't been feeling well so I decided to take time off to help her around the house." She pointed to the shears. "And yard."

He backed away from the shears playfully, but his face had taken on a stricken expression. She knew his concern to be sincere. He must like Mom as much as she liked him.

"Is she all right?"

Elena fidgeted with the shears, grateful for his interest. "I don't know. She's not one to complain, but she hasn't had much stamina for more than a week. With all that's happened in the community, she has me worried."

"Has she seen a doctor?"

Elena shook her head. "I wish, but so far she's made a million excuses and refuses to go. Says she only has a cold and it will clear on its own. She's as single-minded and willful as one of these aphids." She pointed at a trumpet vine with white fuzzy spots and brown curling leaves. "I don't know what to do to move either her or them."

"What if I talked to her?" Adam asked.

"Be my guest, but be prepared for more excuses."

Adam led the way into the living room where Mom was resting on the couch with Sal by her side. As soon as she saw him, she tried to rise, but he held up a hand.

"Don't get up on my account. If you did I wouldn't feel like one of the family."

At this, Mom slumped back down and giggled like a teenager. "We wouldn't want that now would we, Elena?" She flashed Adam a smile that could charm the royal family.

Elena chose to keep her opinion to herself, but her feelings for Adam were definitely not avuncular.

Gabrielle rushed up to Elena and Elena put an arm around her shoulders.

"Hi, Adam," she said.

Adam smiled at her. "Hello, Gabby. How are you?"

"Fine."

Adam took a seat by Mom. "Elena tells me you're not feeling well."

Mom dismissed him with a gesture of her hand. "Not too bad."

"That's not what I hear. She says you've been sick for over a week and haven't seen a doctor."

Mom wagged her head. "She worries about me too much."

Adam gave Elena a knowing look. "Maybe you should see a doctor to make her happy. You don't want her to fret, do you?"

"Well, no." Frieda glanced about as though she were looking for an escape hatch. She had been expertly boxed in. How clever of him. He was certainly proving his worth as a lawyer, and a friend.

"I'm going to LA for a couple of days. If I don't hear from Elena that you've made an appointment by the time I return, I'm going to take you to the doctor myself."

Instead of being surly, which Mom might have done with someone else, she smiled her warmest smile. "All right, Adam, you win."

He sent Elena a triumphant smile.

***

Adam stayed for a cup of coffee, then Elena walked him to his car. He watched while the sun lit a halo around the top of her head. She was an angel all right, an angel of compassion and mercy.

She stood back while he opened the car door. "Remind me to hire you if I ever need a lawyer. In five minutes you accomplished with my Mom what I've failed at for a week."

"I'm well-trained," he said, trying to be modest.

"And you have my mother well-trained, too. She's eating out of your hand." Elena smiled. "By the way, you never told me why you stopped by."

"You're right." Adam leaned over the car, extracted his briefcase and handed her a file. "Thought you might like a copy of the pesticide report for future reference. Even though you readily dismissed it, I think you should take a good look at it."

She took it from him. "I'll read this over."

"Good." He glanced at his watch. "I'm trying to get back to LA early. It's my fiancée's twenty-second birthday. I don't want to be late. I promised her dinner at her favorite restaurant. She was all excited on the phone last night."

He could swear he saw a shadow pass over Elena's face. She diverted her eyes. "What did you buy her?"

"A Coach purse."

"Oh. They're beautiful."

Something in the way Elena said the words made his heart ache. He wanted to understand her sadness, but he wouldn't intrude in her private life. "I'll call you when I come back to see how your mother's doing. Any word yet from the lab?"

Elena's face drooped even more. "Not yet, but I hope soon."

He wished he could stay longer and spend more time with her, but he had promised himself he would be in Los Angeles early and surprise Brittany on her special day. "I'll call when I return to see if your mother followed through."

He folded himself into the Jeep and drove off, glancing into the rearview mirror to watch Elena stare after him. Even from a distance, the sadness in her eyes drew him to her and he had to force himself to look away.

The whole way to LA he had trouble shaking free of his thoughts about Elena, no matter how hard he tried. He kept picturing her staring after him, wind ruffling her shoulder-length hair, caressing her dirt-stained yellow t-shirt. While he would never want to hurt Brittany, he had begun to cherish Elena in an unexpected way, and this was causing him intense conflict.

For one thing, Brittany didn't share his values or his priorities the way Elena did. While he had committed to Brittany and was never one to renege on a promise, he had a nagging feeling his relationship with her wasn't quite right. Perhaps he was lonely after all these days away from Los Angeles and spending time with Brit would ease his confusion.

***

Adam careened into the Budmans' driveway and took the steps to the front door, gleeful he had made the trip in record time. Since the maid had the day off, Irene Budman met him at the door and told him Brittany was still down at the tennis court.

Adam glanced at his watch and noted it was a little after five. He hoped Brit hadn't given up on him and decided to play a set rather than go on their planned private date, no friends allowed. Adam rounded the stately mansion through the side gate and walked down a path overlooking meandering gardens below.

He clutched the box at his side and proceeded to the tennis court to check if Brittany might be about. He ambled past stunning yellow and orange Bird of Paradise and fuchsia flowered jacaranda, past queen palms with vines winding their ways up trunks and came upon the asphalt expanse of the tennis court. Not seeing Brittany, he traipsed past the empty court to the pool area, also abandoned. When he passed the part-stucco, part-bamboo cabana, a sound made him stop and listen.

Shocked, he recognized Brittany's breathless voice say, "Oh yes, yes." Adam couldn't move.

For a long moment, he stood powerless before he quickly got a hold of himself and strode to the cabana door, rapping twice. "Brittany, I know you're in there. Get the hell out here. Now."

A flurry of sounds met his words: a sofa creaking, feet shuffling, voices whispering. Before long the cabana door flew open and Brittany's tennis instructor, Randall, emerged in his tennis whites looking his preppie and sneaky self. "Hey, man, it's not what you think."

"How do you know what I think?" Adam raised his voice in fury. "It's not *you* I want to talk to, it's Brittany. Where is she?"

Brittany ducked her head out the door behind Randall and gave Adam a weak grin. "I wasn't expecting you so early."

"That's obvious."

"Randall was showing me a couple of new moves."

Adam had to stifle a laugh that suddenly gathered in response to her ridiculous lie, which seemed to admit more truth than she had intended. "I'm sure Randall has all the right moves, but you must think I live in a bubble. You've lied. I know what was going on in there."

Brittany blushed a deep scarlet, which would have made her more beautiful in most men's eyes, but not his. For the first time, he could see through her surface glamour and now viewed the ways of her treacherous underbelly. He could kick himself for being so damn superficial and falling for her good looks and outgoing personality. He should have known that anything that looked too good and came too easily had its downside.

"I—I don't know what you mean."

Randall stared from one to the other. "I have a lesson over at the Laramies' at four. I better go."

"I hope Cindy Laramie doesn't require as much private tutoring as Brittany." Adam watched Randall back away, then turn and bolt.

"You really have terrible taste, Brittany. That worm won't even stand by you."

Brittany looked down as her blue eyes filled with tears. He hardened himself against her victim act.

"Adam." She reached for his arm.

He brushed off her hand. "All I want to know is what made you accept my proposal of marriage when you really wanted to be with that snake?" He looked off in the direction Randall had gone.

Brittany continued to stare at the ground and refused to meet his eye. "I love you."

Fury filled him. He grabbed her arms. "Stop the crap, Brittany. You don't love me, and it looks like you never did. For once would you please be kind enough to tell me what's really going on."

"I don't know how you can say that after all I've done for you. Why, I've spent thousands of dollars already on our wedding." She sobbed into an open palm.

"Come on. That has nothing to do with a commitment to me." He lifted her head. "I need to know. Why did you do it?"

Brittany shifted from one foot to the other. "I don't know."

He stood his ground. "No excuses. I want the truth."

She looked past him. "Okay." She sighed. "It was because of Daddy. He was adamant I marry someone in the firm." She glanced up at him. "You know Daddy when he makes up his mind about something."

Cyrus Budman's stubborn streak was legendary, and was probably what made him such a dynamite litigator. It explained how he had managed to work his way up to senior partner in such an established firm. Adam, on the other hand, had been a total patsy, a blind fool who had been led by the nose. Furious with Brittany, he was even angrier with himself. How could he have allowed this to happen? He had always depended on his smarts and instincts to get him by, but he had let himself down. The thought of allowing anyone to know he had been taken sent a shudder of embarrassment through him. He would keep this quiet for a while.

"I'm sorry, Adam."

"How long have you and that loser been seeing each other?"

"Three years." Her eyes again teared. "But Daddy doesn't approve of him. Please don't tell."

"So you were using me to cover your tracks. Thanks a lot."

She hung her head. "I didn't know what else to do. Daddy would have cut off my tennis lessons, sent Randall away if I didn't obey. I thought if I did what he wanted, I could go on..." She covered her mouth with a small, delicate hand.

"Did you ever consider me? My feelings? Or was I a piece on your game board?"

"I really like you Adam, but—"

"But you'll have to do without me as your excuse. Our so-called engagement is off." He spun around and began to stride away, then stopped, returned and handed her the wrapped box. "You might as well take this, it was meant for you. I hope you have a happy birthday."

He marched off in the direction of his new home, Vandasillo.

***

"You're a miracle worker, Adam. You really are." Elena had stopped by Adam's office between morning appointments to tell him her news. He had put his paperwork on hold to speak with her.

"I don't think if I threatened to jump into the well it would have made my mother call that doctor's office. She has an appointment a week from Wednesday."

"Why so far off? Can't they see her sooner?" Adam asked.

Elena shook her lovely head. "I wish. I had to beg for that time. They're booked up. I'm just relieved she's going."

Adam stood and turned to stare out the window. He looked past Lepe's market and the storefront postal station, past the row of parked cars. What he had to ask next was hard. He didn't want to upset Elena, but it couldn't be avoided. "How's your Mom feeling?"

Elena released an audible breath behind him, followed by a sigh. "From what I can tell, she's getting worse. She... Well, she sits around most of the day and lets Gabby, Dad or me do the dirty work. It's so unlike her."

He turned and caught her eye. Worry had etched lines deep into her forehead and around the corners of her mouth. He hated to see her suffer and would have given anything to take her in his arms and ease her pain. She was too good a woman to feel so rotten. "What do you think it is?" He steeled himself against her answer.

"Leukemia." Tears sprang into her eyes. "I know I might be paranoid because of the spate of diseases in this town, but I can't help myself from being afraid for her. I pray every day it's a plain-old viral infection, but it seems to be dragging on so long, and she's so weak and tired, it makes me think this could be a possible diagnosis."

The tears dribbled from the corners of her eyes and leaked onto her cheeks. He could no longer contain himself. He strode around his desk and gathered her into his arms, holding her close to him. When he did, the feel of her soft skin beneath his hands, the scent of her shampoo, the wrenching sound of her sobs made him want to hold onto her and protect her forever. He wanted desperately to take away the pain and fear, but all he could do was press her to him. "I know how you feel. Your mom's an incredible person and a great mother. I'd hate to hear anything like that happening to her or to you."

***

Elena allowed herself to relax against Adam and released the pent-up tears her mother could never see. She had to be strong so much of the time for so many. It felt good to fall apart with him. When the tears subsided, she pulled back and swiped her cheeks. Adam handed her a tissue from his desk and she blotted her eyes. She gave Adam a small smile, not knowing why she trusted him, but she did. Anyone who cared about her mom as much as Adam did was someone she could depend on. "I'll be all right."

He gazed into her eyes. "You don't have to be, and I'd totally understand. I'd be a mess in your shoes. It's really okay to feel what you do."

Elena patted his arm with gratitude for his support. "Thank you," she whispered, fending off more waterworks. Shaky from all the emotion, she took a seat by his desk.

He stood by awkwardly a moment longer before levering himself up on the edge of the desk. "So where to from here?"

"In terms of my mom?"

"For starters."

She rubbed her forehead. "I guess they'll order blood work and whatever else they typically do, then we'll bite our nails and wait for the verdict."

"And?"

She blanched. "And nothing. If she has leukemia, we'll follow the doctor's orders. I don't know what they'll recommend. Chemo? Bedrest? A new home on a different planet? Who knows? Naturally, we'll do everything we can."

A car screeched to a halt outside the window and a man shouted obscenities. Sun flowed through the vertical blinds and sketched lines along the far wall. Children laughed outside the open window. Miraculously, light and life continued on the outside even when it dimmed on her world.

"Hear anything about that water sample?"

"I'm waiting for that, too. My life is one big waiting room right now. I wish I could have the appointment with fate and get it over with."

"I hear you." He picked up an appointment book. "I do have one appointment I have to keep with Harold Rhoades. He called yesterday. Said it was important I meet with him today at two."

She raised a brow. "Oh? What's that about?"

"Don't know, but I'll find out soon enough."

She glanced at her watch and rose. "Enough of my belly-aching for one day. I have OPPs to attend to."

He cocked his head in the boyish way he always did. He was damn adorable. "OPPs?"

"Other People's Problems."

He sent her a small smile. "Ain't that life."

Chapter 10

Outside Adam's office, Elena encountered blinding sunlight and only avoided running into a burly man on the sidewalk by a few inches. He ceased yelling at smaller man, who wrung his hands and kept his eyes down and moved aside to let her pass. When she did, she glanced up to see Herman Molar from the power plant.

"Herman?" she asked tentatively, not wanting to step into the fracas.

Herman squinted his eyes and stared at her. "Hey." He tilted his head to the side. "The lady from the river. Yuse the reason I lost my job. Wait here while I deal with this character. Yuse next."

He turned back to the little man who had managed to scrape together a few dollars from a man standing nearby. "Here you go, José. This might help."

José held out the bills to Herman. "Here, *señor*. Take. *Por favor*."

A crowd had gathered around the two men and a whisper went through it as Herman counted out the money. "A lousy eighty bucks. It'll cost me more to fix this fender." He pointed at an older Buick with a dented rear fender.

The little man's wide eyes pleaded with Herman.

Since José spoke little English, Elena thought she'd better step in. "As far as I know José doesn't have any insurance on his truck. He hasn't been in this country that long. This money is probably all he has in the world except for the truck."

Herman eyed the truck but quickly lost interest. "If I had a job, I'd have no problem payin' for the fender." He turned stormy eyes on her, and she realized he was shaming her for his job loss.

She frowned. "I'm so sorry. I didn't mean to cause you any trouble. How about if I buy you lunch after my next appointment? We can talk this over."

He looked uncertain but stuffed the bills in his pants pocket. Wagging a finger at José, he said, "Watch where yuse going from now on."

José bobbed his head rapidly like one of those dolls with a spring for a neck. "*Si, señor.*" He jumped into his truck, slammed the door and careened off down the street. The crowd slowly scattered.

Herman stared after him, shaking his head. "I hope I did the right thing."

"You did," Elena reassured him. "How about meeting me at El Rancho in an hour. I'll treat you to a bite for all the trouble I've caused you."

"Since all I have is eighty-five dollars in my pocket and that's going for a fender repair, yuse is on."

Before she marched off in the direction of her office, she glanced up at the window above. Adam must have heard the commotion because he stood in the window, his eyes glued on her. She gave him a wave and scurried off to her appointment, already ten minutes late.

After her meeting, Elena went straight to the café. Herman was already seated at a corner table with his back to the wall. He waved her over as soon as he spotted her and watched as she took a seat before gesturing to a waitress. "Hope yuse don't mind. I started without yuse."

A rich aroma rose from the bowl of *sopa* to her nostrils. She inhaled deeply and decided she wanted what he had. "What's that?"

"*Menudo.*" He slurped a large spoonful.

She cringed. Intestines were not her favorite food. Plans revised, she looked over the menu and chose the chicken *tostadas*. The waitress came by and took her order.

With the waitress out of earshot, Elena leaned over the table. Herman continued to make loud slurping sounds that she ignored. "What happened to you? When we met you still had a job."

He placed the spoon down with a clank and grunted. His sounds competed with the noisy lunchtime crowd. "Yuse lied to me. Yuse didn't tell me about snooping around the plant. Rhoades caught wind from one of the other guys that yuse been there and I let yuse take the water. He wanted my head on a platter."

A pang of guilt riveted her to her seat. She didn't know what to say. This poor soul had lost his job because of her. She covered her mouth with a hand. "I'm so sorry. I never meant to bring you into this." Her words sounded ineffectual even to her ears.

He slurped more soup. With the back of his hand, he wiped away a thin line of liquid running down his chin. At least the shock of losing his job hadn't made him lose his appetite. "Whad was yuse doing there anyway that put Rhoades in such a snit?"

She shared with him the trouble in the community and her suspicions. When she finished, he sat back and passed a napkin over his mouth.

"Why didn't yuse tell me that to begin with? Why the cloak and dagger stuff?"

She cast her eyes downward, too ashamed to meet his eyes. "I was afraid you'd give me the heave-ho and I'd never gather my sample."

He sucked on a toothpick and seemed deep in thought.

"I honestly never intended to hurt you," she said. "I'd like to make it up to you."

He sent her a suggestive sideways leer.

She had better set him straight. "What I mean is help you to collect unemployment compensation or find a job."

"Oh." He looked crestfallen.

Elena took a sip of water. The waitress set her plate in front of her. A teenager walking past the window stared at her untouched tostada. She wished she could give it to him since she wasn't terribly hungry after what she'd learned. "Come by my office tomorrow." She rummaged through her purse for her appointment book and then flipped to the next day. "At two. We'll work on setting you up."

"I was about to pack up my pick-up and pull out. Can't pay the rent with nothin' in my pocket." He patted the side of his baggy black pants.

"Where would you go?"

"Back to Jersey where I'm from. Newark. Came out here to work for the power company."

She tried the *tostada*. "I'll be glad to do what I can if you want to stay put. At the very least, I'll sign you up for unemployment compensation. I'll also ask around about work." She took another bite, but had so little appetite she lowered her fork to the plate. "I was wondering if you might know what they do at the plant with the wastewater?"

The spoon he raised toward his mouth stopped in mid-air. "Yuse want me to spill the beans on the plant after all the trouble yuse caused me. Yuse some funny chick." But he wasn't laughing.

"You're no longer at the plant. I thought you could help out the community."

He ate his meal while shaking his head. "Yuse don't think I need references? Listen." He raised his free hand. "I don't know nothin'. I was only security. I can't help yuse with yuse problem."

Elena stared into his eyes and he quickly turned away. She had the distinct sense he knew more than he was saying. It might take time, but she'd find out what he wasn't telling her. She quickly scarfed down a few bites of *tostada* and washed it down with chamomile tea. "Come by my office tomorrow." She handed him her card. "We'll get started."

***

After work, Elena locked the door to her office and carried a pile of papers to the rear of the building toward her car. Before she even reached the vehicle, she noticed glass on the ground by the passenger's side door. She stopped in her tracks and looked up to see that the side window was broken.

She scanned the area to see if the vandal lurked about but didn't see a soul. She crunched over glass shards to her car and surveyed the damage. Her eyes alighted on a scrap of paper attached to a rock lying among more glass on the passenger seat. She opened the car door, reached in for the note with a shaky hand and untied it from the rock. Sprawled across the page in bold lettering were the words, *Leave It Alone.*

She stood gawking at the note for an inordinately long time. When her initial fear subsided, rage rushed through her like a fire through dried sagebrush. She clenched her jaw and stomped her foot. To think Harold Rhoades or one of his cronies would have the audacity to break into her car and try to intimidate her this way was infuriating.

Elena crumbled the paper, but thought better of it, and opened the note, flattening it as best she could. It might be evidence if anything happened to her. Obviously, the power company was playing hardball and it might not stop here.

She took the note, placed it in a pocket and started toward the police station, three blocks away, but didn't make it a full block before she thought about Adam. What if he were in on this stunt. She hated to even think this of him, but he was on their side, after all.

In front of Adam's building, she spied a light in his office window. As usual, he was working late. He should be the first to know about the plant's questionable activities.

She waited in Adam's outer office a good fifteen minutes while he completed a phone consultation and then invited her into his inner sanctum. Shutting the door behind her, she withdrew the note from her pocket and handed it to him. "Someone was nice enough to toss this through my closed car window while I was working."

Adam studied the note, a dark scowl spreading across his boyish features, making him look older than his years. "Someone wants to scare you. Do you know who?"

"I have three guesses. The power company, the power company, the—"

"Let me try. The power company, right?"

"Exactly."

He glanced again at the note. "I don't buy it. This is from an irate or frightened person. It's too adolescent for a big company. They might be good old boys, but they wouldn't stoop to these tactics."

"Who else would want to scare me off?"

He handed the note back to her, still hovering over his desk. She pocketed it.

"You counsel a number of dysfunctional families with complicated interpersonal problems. Perhaps one of them wants you off their back."

She slid into the seat by his desk and sighed. "Perhaps, but for some reason all I could think of when I saw this was the power company. It smacks of their manipulation. I heard from an ex-employee that the executives know I took a water sample from the stream near the plant. Maybe I'm being overly suspicious, but they'd have a motive for wanting me off their case."

Adam leaned forward, elbows on the desk, expression serious. "I'm only concerned that if someone is harassing you, they'd be willing to up the ante. You need to report this incident to the police if you haven't already. Take precautions, especially since we don't know who it is."

"What kind of precautions?"

"Like not placing yourself in a vulnerable position. You shouldn't be out alone. Park in public places. Do everything you can to be safe."

She gave him an exasperated expression, although deep down she really appreciated his concern. "I won't be a prisoner in my own town."

"I'm not asking you to hide out in your home, only to take necessary precautions. If you have to go somewhere by yourself, I'll be happy to escort you."

Her heart swelled with gratitude for his support. Most of the kids she grew up with had either left Vandasillo as soon as they could for the big city or were back in Mexico. Since she couldn't tell her family what was going on, Adam might be her only true support system in town. The irony of this didn't escape her. "I might take you up on your offer."

His eyes held hers for a moment longer than was necessary and a shiver ran through her.

"Just put your lips together and whistle."

She moistened her mouth with the tip of her tongue and blew air between her slightly opened lips. No sound escaped.

***

Adam dropped Elena off at the sheriff's station and insisted on waiting for her. Inside, a lone officer leaned back in his chair with tooled boots atop the metal desktop. He listened intently to a Dodgers game on the radio. As soon as the screen door slammed shut behind Elena, he swung his legs down and came to attention by his desk. With a quick reach, he turned down the radio.

"Can I help you?"

Elena glanced around the tiny substation that had room for only two desks and an old metal filing cabinet. A couple of local maps hung on the wall. A large round clock over the desk read six-thirty. Although she had called home from Adam's office to say she'd be late, she wanted to keep this as short as possible.

She produced the note and told the officer what had happened. As she spoke he filled out a report, taking down all the details as well as her personal information.

When he was through taking notes, he tossed the report in a folder. "Is your car parked nearby?"

"Behind the County Social Service office on Main."

"Lead me to it and let's take a look."

After letting Adam know she was in safe hands, Elena rode with the cop to her car and watched while he walked around and entered more notes in the file. "Will you take any fingerprints?"

He gave her a look that suggested she might be watching too many police shows. "They probably threw the rock and never touched the car. Fingerprints won't prove anything except who's been riding with you lately." He wrote down the plate and VIN numbers. "That's all I'll need for now. Call back tomorrow and I'll have a report prepared for your insurance company."

"What will happen with the investigation?"

He frowned. "Right now we don't have any leads and you're not even sure who could have done this." He pointed at the broken window. "Until we have more to go on than hearsay, we'll file this away."

"But what if my suspicions are right and it is an executive at the power company?"

"Look, Miss. We're not going to bother Mr. Rhoades or anyone at the company without any evidence. Now, if you come up with something more substantial, then we'd be glad to follow up."

She bit back the question that sprang into her mind, but couldn't help wondering how much money the power company gave to the sheriff's annual fundraiser. She had hoped the police presence would alert Rhoades they were on his tail, but that didn't appear to be a possibility. "Whoever did this might not stop here."

"If you have any more trouble, report it immediately to us. Call the emergency number any time morning, noon or night. We always have a dispatcher on duty."

That sounded about as lame as Pacheco's horse, but what had she expected? If she had another incident, by the time she could inform the police, who knew what might transpire? "I'll do that. *Adios*."

The officer saluted her and drove off, leaving Elena in his dust.

She stood looking at her smashed window for a long time, trying to tamp down the fear and frustration before she went home. Since the driver's side was untouched, she could drive home and clean the car later. She would tell her family the damage had been done by a teenage vandal on the prowl. She didn't want to worry them.

She'd never let them know she may be at risk.

Chapter 11

"Sorry, that's outside of our service area," the owner of the mobile window replacement company in Fresno said.

"I understand that." Adam doodled with the sun's face on the yellow-page ad. "What if I paid extra for your time and mileage?"

"Hum." Silence filled the phone and then the owner said, "I'll see what I can do. It depends on the boys. If one of them wants to drive down there, you're on."

"How soon will you know?"

"I'll call back by this afternoon. Leave me your number."

Adam gave him the information. "By the way, I'd appreciate it if you wouldn't mention that I paid for the replacement. She'd probably turn it down. Is that okay?"

The owner's muffled voice gave orders to someone else, then he said, "What do we tell her when she asks?"

"That it's a gift from someone who cares. Don't say anything more."

"Sure. You're the one footing the bill. I'll give you a holler later."

Adam replaced the receiver. If Elena knew he had arranged for her window repair, she might interpret it as a bribe, the last thing he intended. He only wanted to be there for her, especially with so much going on in her life, but right now he had to lay low and keep business separate from friendship.

***

Elena had taken an early lunch break to scour Fresno's yellow pages for a window repair service. She could arrange to have the repair done when she drove her mother to her doctor's appointment, otherwise, she'd never find the time. Grateful that the weather was still warm enough to drive around with an open-air vehicle, she flipped through the pages.

A knock at the office door pulled her away from her search. She opened to find a man in jeans and a white work shirt with yellow lettering that read "Window Repair and Replacement." The man held out a card. "I'm here to replace a passenger-side window on a Toyota Tercel. Are you Elena Markeys?"

"Yes, I'm Elena Marquez, but I'm confused. I never called you."

The man grinned. "Nope. Says here someone called in but doesn't give their name. Asked us to replace that window of yours."

Stunned, Elena was speechless. She shook her head to shake off the strange feeling. "That's awfully nice of whoever it is, but how much do you charge?"

The man held a hand in front of her face. "The bill's been taken care of. All you have to do is sign here." He held out a form attached to a clipboard and pointed to a blank line.

Still thrown off-kilter by this sudden change of plans, Elena felt as though she had mistakenly stepped into a parallel universe where everything was similar but different. Like after she took her car to the mechanic and her seat had been moved, and her mirror shifted. Nonetheless, she signed the form.

"Where's the patient?" the man asked, taking back the clipboard, detaching the form and slipping it into a file.

"Out back. I'll take you there."

"No problem." He began to toward the door. "I'll find it, I can't miss. It's the one with the broken window, right?" He smiled broadly. "I'll let you know when I'm done."

"You might need this." Elena tossed him the key. He smiled, walked out and closed the door. From the window, she watched him survey the parking area in case he had trouble locating the car. Her mother and father were amazing—this was so much like them. She would have to give them both big hugs when she went home.

***

"I don't believe you. It's not that I don't appreciate your generosity, but you shouldn't have done that."

Elena stood in the entrance to Adam's office, hands on her hips. The dark scowl on her face bewildered him. His intention had been only to please her, make up for the violation, not anger her.

He waved her into the office. "Close the door behind you and have a seat. No use letting everyone know our problems."

She did as he asked but sat perched on the edge of the chair. "I don't understand what this is all about. If you think for one second you can use this window repair as a way to sway me to your side, you have another thought coming."

He held up his hands. "That wasn't at all what I intended. All I wanted to do was help you out. I really didn't mean anything devious or manipulative."

"Then why didn't you ask me first? Don't you realize you stepped over a line?"

He lowered his eyes. "I'm sorry. I simply hated to see you so traumatized. I wanted to be a friend and do something to cheer you up. You and your family have been so good to me. I thought that was the least I could do."

Slowly, she shook her head from side to side. "I know you might be innocent, but you went too far with this. I'm uncomfortable with the whole arrangement. I insist on paying for the repairs." She reached toward her purse by her side.

Adam stepped around the desk and propped himself on the edge, facing her. "You don't understand. You've already paid me more than this could ever cost. You and your family have fed me meals and befriended me at a time when I didn't know a soul in town. What I did in no way approaches the value of what you've given me." His eyes caught hers and held. Pink tinged her cheeks and she looked away.

"I'm sorry, Adam, but I have to pay you back."

He looked down at her. "With what? Aren't you already overextended with the laboratory fees? That's another reason I paid for the window repair. I knew it would be harder for you than me to come up with the money right now."

He had a point. "Is this also a way of admitting the power company is at fault?"

He jerked his head up. "I'm not saying anything of the sort. That had nothing to do with my actions. I told you why I did it."

She bit her lip. "Okay. I'll tell you what. Since you're right, I'm a few pennies overextended, I'll have to postpone paying you back, but don't worry, I'll do it."

"I'm really not worried. And one way you could pay me back is by taking me on that hike you promised."

She hesitated then nodded. "I can arrange that, but I'll also find a way to pay for the window repair. I won't let you obligate me in any way. I want to be free to make up my own mind."

Her strength and determination always impressed him. "You're as independent as they come, Elena. That's a given."

***

At first, Elena had been pleased with Adam's remark. Only later had she scoffed at his words. *Independent as they come.* He hadn't seen her with Ron. She had overstayed that relationship by years. Every time she'd tried to end things, Ron was there with an apology and an excuse and she would be persuaded to take him back. Not so much for herself, but for Gabby, she would ignore her doubts. She had denied or justified his behavior until she no longer could, and that now made her feel like a fool. She would never want to be fooled again, even by Adam Slater.

She chuckled to herself. Why would she even consider Adam a potential suitor since it was out of the realm of possibilities? The only conceivable reason was that he had all the qualities she could ever want in a man. He was warm and generous, bright and interesting, and good to her and her family. Even with her suspicions, the more she grew to know him, the more she grew to like him. He possessed all the traits Ron lacked. Where Ron was self-obsessed and infantile, Adam seemed concerned and attentive. Where Ron snubbed her parents and didn't have time for Gabby, Adam showed genuine interest in them.

Yes, Adam had everything she could possibly want in a man, except his lack of availability. Now she had to draw the line in her own mind about him and not allow herself to ruminate on the impossible.

The only problem: her heart had a mind of its own.

Chapter 12

The trail cut through pine and spruce before it began a steep hillside ascent. Adam relished the fresh evergreen fragrance of the mountain air, the cool breeze on his cheeks. Being in the mountains was like nowhere else on earth, at least in this part of the planet.

He slowed his pace to allow Elena to catch up before he followed a series of switchbacks to the crest of the hill. When he reached the top and rounded the bend, the trail dipped before continuing its relentless climb.

"Whew." He took a bandana from his jeans pocket and wiped his brow.

"I told you this trail wasn't for wimps." Elena gave him a wide grin and offered him a drink from the bottle hung from a shoulder strap.

He took a swig, then poured water into his hands to rub across his nape. "No one's ever called me a wimp. Let's carry on."

"Hold your horses, I could use a short break. The waterfall is only about two miles ahead, but it's an uphill battle."

She lowered herself onto an outcropping of rock and he joined her. She took another sip of water, capped the bottle and set it aside in the shade. "This canyon is beautiful, isn't it?"

He glanced around, taking in the splendor of the surrounding peaks and valleys, then caught himself staring at Elena. Her long dark hair had been pulled back to reveal deeply ridged cheek-bones, more distinctive than the crevices between the ridges, and full unpainted lips. Her high forehead suggested a woman of depth and intelligence, qualities he admired.

"I could live in these woods if I could only make a living here. Unfortunately, there aren't enough bears who need legal services to pay for a barrister."

She kept her eyes averted under his stare. "How about Smokey? He must have had some cash. All that advertising."

"But he's gone. How many bears have you seen on television lately?"

"Barely any." She beamed at her own joke.

He gave her a playful cuff to the shoulder and groaned. "Bad, Marquez."

"You'll bear up," she said, and grinned wider.

"Ugh. No more unbearable humor, please."

The sun peeked out from behind a cloud and warmed them. Elena lay back and stretched her long legs over the side of the outcropping. "So tell me about you."

"What's there to tell? I was born and reared in LA. Malibu, to be exact."

She peered at him, a hand shielding her eyes from the sun. "You must be from money."

"My parents are real estate developers. They made a few bucks, especially during the booms of the late eighties and nineties. A couple of really good investments took them a long way. You know the score, although it was hard to make a bad investment in the California market at the time."

"And you?"

"I did my undergrad at UCLA, then after a few years teaching middle school, I went to Stanford. Goodman, Lubbock, Weingard and Budman recruited me fresh out of law school and I've been with them for the last two years."

She kept her half-closed eyes on his face. "How'd you meet your fiancée?"

"Brittany?" He had the urge to tell her he no longer had a fiancée, but this didn't seem the time for a lengthy explanation. He was still too embarrassed by his obvious error of judgment and didn't feel safe sharing it yet. For someone who graduated at the head of his law school class, he had made a pretty idiotic mistake.

"I met her at the firm's Christmas party. She was the prettiest and most vivacious girl in the room. That was six months ago." Little did he know at the time that Brittany vivacious translated to rarely a moment alone without friends and also meant self-centered and demanding. The traits that originally attracted him had become the exact ones that ended up irking him. But wasn't that often the case.

"Congratulations." She sat up. "Time to hit the trail."

"Wait one minute. You've managed to extract my entire life story from me. What about you?"

"We'll have time at the falls."

Elena began to trek up the hill with Adam trailing behind until the next set of switchbacks. Then she fell behind. He had trouble reining in his steps to keep from losing her. Every so often he had to stop to allow her to catch up. When he reached the latest plateau, he looked out over purple mountain peaks crowned with trees and a deeply etched, verdant river valley below.

Behind him, he heard Elena say, "Why not take a picture, it lasts longer."

"Good idea." He settled his day pack on a rock and pulled out his Minolta with the wide-angle lens to capture the panoramic view. After snapping the photograph he turned the lens in Elena's direction.

She threw her hands over her face, laughing. "Nooooo."

"Don't be shy. Come on. Show your face, Marquez, and say cheese."

Slowly, she lowered her hands, struck a silly pose and said, "*Queso.*"

He took the shot and had the unexpected sense he'd always cherish it.

"Now you," she said.

"I'm totally un-photogenic."

"Prove it." She tried to free the phone from his grip and he held firm. When he finally released it, she stumbled backward. Quickly, he reached out and clasped her to him to break her fall. Pressed against him, she felt so warm and right.

She levered herself away with a hand on his chest. "I'll be fine." Then she brushed herself off. "Now stand over there." She pointed at a rock outcropping.

He stepped toward the rock and looked down at the sheer drop. "A-ha. Now I know your plan. You say, one step backward and I'm over the side. A neat way to rid yourself of a nuisance."

"I know you're an attorney, but would you stop talking, Slater. Give it a break and show that expensive dental work."

He put on his best picture-taking smile and she took the shot.

"Good, now move back a little bit."

He shook his finger at her. "Too late, I'm on to you." He checked the level of the sun on the horizon. "Must be at least four. Let's hoof it, or we'll be groping our way back in the dark."

"Groping? Not me I hope." She sent him a wry smile. "Don't worry. It takes half the time going down. I promise I'll have you back before dark."

He placed his phone back in his rear jeans pocket. "Lead the way, José."

Farther down the trail it narrowed and at times almost disappeared. He had to stay close to the rock face or fall over the side. At last, the trail opened onto a flat meadow and they meandered past fields of yellow, blue and orange wildflowers.

"When does this end?" he asked over his shoulder.

"We don't have much farther."

Her definition of "much farther" was different from his as they traveled through another mountain pass with a serious uphill climb. Finally, the trail became slick and rocky, indicating water ahead. He heard the falls' babble long before they reached it and the sound slowly amplified from a gurgle to a gush to a roar. Around a bend, he beheld a magnificent sight. Looking up, he saw water pour over a mountaintop. It tumbled and cascaded over huge boulders straight down to a fast-flowing stream full of foam-capped waves.

"Wow," he yelled at Elena, whose response was drowned out by the rushing water.

She caught up with him. "Follow me to the riverbed."

He did as she said and stepped over slick twigs and roots to the stream below. There, sheltered by a grove of cottonwood, they took side-by-side seats on a large fallen tree limb.

They again shared a swig from the bottle and leaned back to rest against a rock.

Adam gave Elena a few minutes to catch her breath. The sun had warmed her caramel-colored cheeks to a rosy glow and her eyes sparkled. "You can't wiggle off the hook a second time. It's your turn to tell me about you."

She grimaced. "I knew as a lawyer you'd never drop the case, but my life is so… so uneventful. I don't even know where to start."

"How about at the beginning."

She rolled her eyes. "You sure you want to hear this?

"Shoot."

"Okay. I was born in Nicaragua and moved to Imperial Valley with my parents when I was six. My father had been working in the fields and managed to put a few dollars away to purchase a tiny old travel trailer from its owner, which was when we moved up here. All five of us lived in that trailer and were we cramped, but we never complained. It was better than what we had in Nicaragua." She looked at him. "Bored yet?"

"Not at all. Go on."

"We worked hard, all of us in the fields. My parents, me and my two brothers, every moment we had before and after school, weekdays and weekends, until we had saved enough to buy a small, arid piece of land to move the trailer onto."

"How'd they allow you to work so young?"

"At first, I helped my mother. She took in laundry, sewing, did housecleaning in Fresno, whatever she could get. I tagged along. Later, I worked alongside my father in the fields. We did whatever job we had to."

"When did you become a citizen?"

She took another draw from the bottle. "Do you remember when the illegals were given citizenship in the late seventies if they'd been working in the U.S. for a time and could prove it? My folks had the farm by then and were able to put together enough money from a bumper crop, along with borrowing from relatives to pay the legal fees."

He raised a brow. "I know legal fees, and that must have been quite a stretch for them."

"They were determined that we all become citizens. They didn't want any of us to face the same threat of deportation they lived under for so many years." She had a far-off look in her eyes. "Not long after that, my oldest brother, Arturo Junior, left to join the service. He lives in Texas now with his wife and two kids. My other brother, Javier, moved to Portland, Oregon."

"How about you?"

"I finished high school as valedictorian and went on to UCLA on scholarship. After graduate school in social work I married my college sweetheart, Ron, found a job with the county, and settled in Glendale."

His curiosity was piqued. "Sounds cozy. What happened to Ron?"

She toyed with her hands.

To comfort her, he placed a hand over hers.

"Sorry. I can't think about Ron without having a reaction." She patted his hands and removed hers.

He could still feel the warmth of her. "Why?"

She hesitated a long moment. "While we were dating he was the epitome of kindness and gentleness, but as soon as we were married, he became critical and demanding. It's like I dated Dr. Jekyll and married Mr. Hyde. I couldn't believe the overnight transformation."

She gnawed at her bottom lip.

This must be hard for her. If he knew her better, and if they weren't fighting a legal battle, he'd be tempted to place an arm around her and comfort her.

"I found out I was pregnant with Gabby when I was planning to leave him. So I put my plans on hold. Even though he'd say mean things to me, I justified his behavior because he had problems at work and was unhappy. My job and the baby kept me distracted from the problems with Ron."

Her eyes misted. "Then one night, when Gabby was three, he raised a hand to strike her. At that moment, I knew we had to go. His nastiness with me was one thing, but his hitting her was quite another. I had to protect her. I found a comfy apartment in Anaheim and moved in."

"Did you think of returning to Vandasillo then?"

"Of course, but I still had my job and Gabby was in preschool. I had already disrupted her world once with the move away from Ron. I wanted to keep the rest of her routine intact. In the meantime, my brother, Javier, had moved back in with my folks to get his life together. They had enough stress without Gabby and me. Besides, things seemed to settle down for a while. Ron met a new woman and my life was full. But then Ron broke off his relationship and began to stalk me. He'd show up at my door at unexpected times, waited for me if I wasn't home, left threatening messages—it was a nightmare."

She hesitated, stared at the ground. "And you know what's most ironic?"

"What?"

"Ron had taken a job at Valley View Gas and Electric's main plant in LA Country. He started as an electrical engineer and worked his way up the ranks to director of operations."

"Whoa. Does that mean he has some type of administrative relationship with the Vandasillo branch?"

"Not directly, that I know of anyway, but the board of directors oversees both plants."

"So how did you end up back in Vandasillo?"

Her voice became strained, and the hand that she combed through her hair quivered. "I always knew I'd be back someday, but I didn't know how soon. I wanted to work with the migrants here—it's the place where I began—but first I had a job to do in Los Angeles."

She glanced off into the distance. "Now you know everything about me. We're from completely different worlds, you and I."

His heart went out to her. He thought he'd had it tough with his absent parents, but his life was an amusement park ride compared to hers. "We can still be friends."

"Perhaps. But there's a huge mountain of difference to crest." She glanced at her watch. "We better head back, it's almost dusk. My mom's looking after Gabby. She insisted I need the break." She started to push herself up.

He stopped her with a hand on her arm. "You know, you're quite a woman."

The look in her eyes went from surprised to pleased.

Then she turned away. "I don't know. I certainly made my share of mistakes. I placed Gabriella in harm's way."

"But you sincerely care about others and want to help them."

She nodded, deep in thought.

He had never met a woman as caring and unselfish as Elena Marquez, and probably wouldn't again.

***

By the time they reached the Marquez house the sky had turned navy blue and, without streetlights, the car interior was dark. Elena noticed a lone light in the kitchen window. She opened the car door to trigger the interior dome light and turned to Adam. "Want to come in for a cup of coffee before you go home? My folks are still up."

"Are you sure it's okay?" he asked. "You know, with your mother under the weather. I don't want to put her out or tire her."

"Actually she seems to be doing a bit better. We have the doctor's appointment next week and I'll know more at that time. "

"Then I'd love to come in." Adam opened his door and followed her into the house.

In the kitchen, her mother stood by the stove stirring a pot of simmering *chiles* while her father sat at the table reading a paper. He looked up as they entered the room.

"You look like something Sal dragged in."

Elena collapsed into a chair after offering Adam a seat. "Sal wouldn't give me a second look."

As if in confirmation, Sal poked his nose up from under the table, sniffed the air and immediately put his head back down. Dad laughed heartily.

Mom gave Adam her sweetest smile. The way her mother smiled at Adam, Elena could swear her mother had already adopted him. Elena wasn't certain how having him as an adopted brother made her feel.

"Good to see you, Adam."

Adam smiled back. "Good to be seen after the horrors of Elena's hike. I wasn't sure I'd make it back."

Dad chuckled with him. "She's a slave driver. How about a cup of coffee? That should perk you up."

"Is there ever a time coffee isn't brewing in this house?" Adam stood and turned his chair so that the back rested against the table.

"Only when there's a funeral and it's one of us." Dad laughed. "Otherwise you can come by at three in the morning for a cup."

Mom handed Adam a mug and turned to Elena. "And you?"

"I'll pass."

"Elena tells us you're a hot-shot lawyer with a big law firm," Mom said.

Elena's face heated at her mother's remark, but she refused to wither under Adam's quizzical gaze.

"She's exaggerating. The firm's big—I'm not," he said.

"I don't know about that." Dad raised his head and looked up at Adam in a pronounced way. "You look pretty big to me." He laughed his husky belly laugh and Mom joined in.

"Maybe we're too short to say." Mom laughed.

Warm fuzzies filled Elena at her parents' silly but loving exchange. "They're incorrigible. They refuse to grow up and act like the miserable, boring adults they're supposed to be. Can you believe them?"

"Are you kidding? I want to be just like them when I grow up and be as happy with my wife and family. I'm green with envy." Adam pointed at his green t-shirt.

Dad roared. "Then you'll be the Jolly Green Giant."

She couldn't believe her ears. This had gone too far. She put on an exasperated expression. "You asked for that one, Adam. That will teach you not to even try and make jokes around here. You open yourself up to competition."

"I'm fair game. No one's off limits in this house."

"Only those we can't trust." Elena knew her mother's remark referred to Ron.

"Don't tell me there's anyone you don't like," Adam said.

"Oh, you'd be surprised," Dad replied. "We're picky, aren't we? That's why we let that thief, Alonso, borrow our tractor. We'll probably never see it again."

Mom wagged a finger at him. "Don't say *we*. That was all your idea. You wanted to be the big man."

Dad turned to Elena. "It's never your mother's idea. Even you kids. It was all me."

"But I helped out," Mom quipped.

Dad reached out and gave her a pat on the rear.

Elena didn't know whether to join in with a wisecrack or hide her head. Her parents were so unpredictable and not at all restrained.

Adam stood. She wondered if he was uncomfortable with their uninhibited behavior, but his eyes sparkled with enjoyment.

"I wish I didn't have to go so soon." He pushed his empty mug toward Mom. "I have work to do in the morning."

Mom lifted the mug. "Are you sure you have to go?"

"Sorry."

"You will come again soon. You're always welcome here," Mom said.

"I'll take you up on that."

Elena walked him to the door, but before he left, he turned to her and took her hand. His dwarfed hers with his long, thick fingers and warm touch.

"I wanted to tell you what a wonderful day I had today. We'll have to do this again."

In the semi-dark, his face remained shrouded in shadow, but Elena could sense a current of some sort pass between them. *Forbidden pleasure.* She squeezed his hand. "We will," and then closed the door behind him.

***

Too restless to sleep, Elena paced the floor of her bedroom. She glanced at her clock: two in the morning. All she could think about was Adam, but he was in another place, fantasizing about a different woman.

She picked up her latest book club selection and tried to read, but she couldn't complete a paragraph without visualizing Adam on the plateau or silhouetted against the gushing waterfall. She put aside the book. No use fooling herself. This man unsettled her in a way no one else ever had, not even Ron.

She had been young when she'd met her ex, but she was a woman now. A woman with needs and desires. And every need and desire she had led her straight to Adam Slater. Why couldn't she have picked someone like Adam for a husband?

She wrapped an old, ratty-yellow terrycloth robe around her, slipped into furry slippers Gabby had chosen for their plastic eyes and sewn-on Cheshire cat grin and padded, as quietly as she could, into the kitchen. Much to her surprise, her mom sat in the half-light that streamed through the window from the full moon.

"What are you doing up?" Mom asked.

"I haven't been able to sleep. Thought I'd have a cup of warm milk like mother used to make."

Her mother stood. "Sit, *mija*. Let me mother you again. I need the practice."

Elena stood aside to let Mom pass. "How can you be out of practice? You're a pro." Her mother opened the refrigerator. In the swatch of light that escaped, Elena could see the strain on her face. "I'm surprised to see you up. Anything wrong?"

Mom closed the door with a toe and carried the milk carton to the counter. "I took a long nap this afternoon. Probably too long. I can't go back to sleep."

This worried Elena. "Another nap? What's going on?"

Mom put the milk in a pan on the stove. "It's really nothing serious."

Her appointment to see a doctor in Fresno was still a week away. Elena didn't know if she could wait that long. "You'd tell me the truth and not try to protect me, wouldn't you?"

"Of course."

Elena knew better. "I hope so."

Mom stirred the milk. "What's turned you into a night owl?"

"Guess I have too much on my mind to sleep."

With a towel, Mom removed the pan from the fire. "Not Ron, I hope?"

"Nah. That's passed. Other things."

Mom poured the milk into a cup and gave it to her along with a small wry smile. "Is it Adam?"

Her mother's ability to see through her always caught Elena by surprise. She groaned. "I told you he's taken. Why would you ask that?"

Mom slumped into a seat. "Taken or not, he's a handsome man and you're an available woman with feelings."

Elena sipped the warm milk, letting the comfort flow down her throat, trying to think of a comeback. "I might be available, but he isn't. Besides, after Ron, I took a moratorium on relationships. I don't exactly know how to pick 'em."

"Remember, *mija*, he looked good for a while with his big job in Los Angeles. We all thought you had married well." Mom sat forward. "Besides, it's never too late to dream."

Elena rose. "I can only dream if I go to sleep." She bent over and kissed her mother on the forehead. "And you need your shut-eye too, or how will you keep up with Gabby in the morning? Get some sleep and I'll see you tomorrow."

Elena dragged herself back to her bedroom, careful not to spill the milk she placed on the nightstand. She slid herself into the bed, then flicked off the light.

Being up half the night pining for a soon-to-be-married man was insane. She would have to keep her emotional distance from him and make sure their relationship remained all work and no temptation.

Chapter 13

Adam drove his Jeep into town, but rather than stop at his apartment—really, the two back rooms of the Ortega house he called an apartment—he kept driving. He was too restless to turn in for the night. He headed out on the 215 north toward Fresno, the city a muted glow in the distance. The moonlight and car beams barely defined the sagebrush and other shrubs along the flat unlit stretch of highway.

Bright beacons of light flashed past him. He drifted to the right to allow them to pass. In no rush, he needed the leisurely pace to think. The frightening thought that he wanted to be more than a friend to Elena had begun to form in his mind. He tried to dispel the images of her that popped into his head: the wise eyes that crinkled at the corners when she smiled, the slim fingers that caressed the water bottle, the long hair that swayed with her every step. He wanted to shut out her voice that flowed like melted butter over him, rich and inviting. Most of all, he wanted to stop the zinging that charged through him with every thought of her.

His gut wrenched. He had made a commitment to the power plant, and he took it seriously. Having more than a friendship with Elena would be a conflict of interest. Besides, he had only recently ended his engagement. He was hardly ready to begin another relationship. Yet, no matter how hard he tried to suppress thoughts of the beautiful, fiery woman, they kept coming, unbidden.

He rubbed his eyes. The clock said eleven-thirty: time to head back into town. As he turned the car around facing south, he questioned why she'd begun to plague him so. What was it about her he found so appealing? Her exotic looks were alluring, but there was something powerfully magnetic about her, something inexplicably attractive. Could it be her compassion for others, or her willingness to fight for a cause and stand up for what she believed in? He didn't know many other people who would risk their pleasures and property to do what she did. Most of the folks he socialized or worked with put the acquisition of objects before their concern for people. He admired Elena for having her priorities straight.

But admiration was a far cry from love, wasn't it?

Yet, he couldn't ignore the way he felt.

***

Harold Rhoades gave Adam a hard stare. "I don't know what Ms. Marquez thinks she's going to accomplish, but she's becoming a nuisance to the functioning of our company. She was recently seen lunching with an ex-employee and rumors are flying. She's affecting employee morale. She seems to be fixated on exposing us as felons. For some unknown reason, she has a bee in her bonnet about the plant. Maybe she's still upset we didn't hire one of her friends. Who knows. What's your take on this?"

Adam sensed what Rhoades wanted him to say, but he couldn't give him the satisfaction and risk Elena's reputation and good works. "She's doing what she thinks is best."

"Listen, Adam. If Marquez has her way, I believe she'd shut us down. Then where would the community be? No power. Ha. I'm sure they'd love that." Rhoades narrowed his eyes even more. "Besides, a lot of good people depend on this company for their livelihoods. I don't think they'd take well to her interference."

"Someone has already threatened Ms. Marquez with a note attached to a rock that was tossed through her car window."

Rhoades shrugged. "I'm sorry to hear that, but she's brought it on by making a pest of herself. I don't know what we have to do to discourage her unnecessary and irresponsible behavior, but she's overdoing this detective stuff especially since we're not the bad guys."

Adam saw the flash of anger quickly spread across Rhoades's face, then just as quickly dissipate. The anger mirrored his own outrage at Rhoades's inferred threat to Elena's safety. "If you have nothing to hide, why don't you just ignore her?"

The phone rang and Rhoades answered it. While he spoke, Adam glanced at the diplomas on the wall behind his desk. A master's degree in business from Harvard next to a commendation from Governor Gray Davis was framed in gold. Next to that hung a photograph of Rhoades at the White House shaking hands with President G.W. Bush. Rhoades certainly had all the pedigrees and society's stamp of approval.

Rhoades hung up the phone. "Sorry. The governor wants a report on our production for the legislature by next Tuesday. Can't keep him on hold." Rhoades looked confused. "Now where were we?"

"I was saying if Ms. Marquez doesn't uncover anything worthwhile, she'll eventually give up and go away."

"I'm not certain of that. Her type's a tenacious dog with a bone. She'll hang on until she unearths a small splinter and then act like it's a forest. She could really embarrass us and cause dissension in the ranks. I don't want to risk that. I want her off our backs. That's why I hired you in the first place."

Adam raised a brow. "I wasn't aware of that. I thought I was hired to represent your interest, not eliminate your enemy. And how do you propose I move that mountain?"

"You know, Adam," Rhoades said in a patronizing tone that raised his hackles. "You're the lawyer here. You're being paid, handsomely, I might add, to take care of this little irritation. You figure out how to deal with her."

Adam had to swallow the urge to strangle this man. "Do you have any further reports or information that would help to support your position?"

Rhoades turned red. "Haven't I already given you enough ammunition to blow away an army? Use what you have, man, and get rid of her."

Frustration caused Adam to tense and a muscle throbbed under his eye. "I don't think it will be that simple." He grabbed a paper off his briefcase and wadded it into a ball. "She's not a piece of paper you can toss aside because she annoys you." He tossed it across the desk into a wastepaper basket and was impressed with his aim. "She's a sharp and strong woman. Don't underestimate her."

Rhoades's eyelids hooded over and Adam couldn't tell what he was thinking.

"Perhaps your firm has overestimated you. I placed a call to Douglass Lubbock this afternoon to let him know the trouble we've run into here. If something doesn't change soon, we may have to ask him to replace you with a different attorney."

Adam froze, the threat no longer hidden. If he didn't do exactly what Rhoades wanted, he was out, not only here, but at the firm. He was too new to survive this level of humiliation. His career as an attorney would be doomed. He would be relegated to drunk driving and domestic violence cases until the day he died. "I've been on this assignment for three weeks. Let me see what I can do before you speak with Lubbock. I'll report back to you as soon as I make headway."

Rhoades sent him an anemic smile. "That's the attitude I'm looking for. Positive. Aggressive." He stood and walked Adam to the door, patting him on the shoulder. "I know you're going to be a fine lawyer, and you can start proving it right here and now."

Outside the power plant, Adam took his time walking to his car, torn in half. His feelings for Elena vied with his desire to do his job and be the best attorney he could be. While he wanted to protect her with all his heart, his whole future hung on how he handled this assignment. And it meant obstructing everything Elena did. He ached with the thought of abandoning her to the wolves.

Then he considered Rhoades's pat on the back. Funny, he had spent most of his life trying to garner approval from other men. His father. His friend's fathers. His teachers. His boss. Now, at last, he had a real chance to please a man who could help him advance in his career, and Adam felt revulsion and resistance. Something significant had changed.

And he wasn't certain how to define it.

***

Adam sat across from Elena at a café in Fresno. Since she had to visit a client there, and he had business in town at the same time, he had urged her to meet him face to face for a cup of coffee.

She stirred the steaming liquid. "So, why the urgency?"

Adam looked drained. There were bags under his eyes and lines etched his forehead. "No urgency. I thought since we were both going to Fresno..."

"Mmm-hmm." She sensed this was something more than a friendly get together. He had seemed determined to see her when he'd called earlier. "So spill."

Adam sighed. "I don't know how to tell you this, but Harold Rhoades is adamant that the power company has no fault in any of the local problems. He's insistent that I convince you of their innocence and that I persuade you to look somewhere else for the culprit. He doesn't want to see or hear from you anymore."

Elena put her cup down with a thud. "Well, I don't give a rat's ass what Harold Rhoades wants or doesn't want. What I want is the truth at any cost."

"At any cost? How about the cost to your safety, and the safety of your family?"

She blinked in astonishment. Was he really threatening her and her family? It was so out of character, she could hardly believe it. "Are you threatening me?"

"Not me. But if you continue your investigation who knows what Rhoades might do. I wouldn't put anything past him."

"And you? Why are you the bearer of such good cheer? What did Rhoades offer you to get me off his back?"

He shook his head. "Nothing. I'm worried about you. I don't want you to be hurt."

"I'm a big girl and I can take care of myself, thank you. I don't need your concern."

He took her hand. "Don't fool yourself. Rhoades has the money and the power to make your life miserable...or worse."

She sat back and studied him. His plea had caused beads of sweat to pop up on his forehead, and his face had turned a deep red. Her discomfort suddenly turned to disdain. He had sold out to the company. He had lost her respect.

"You didn't answer me. What did Rhoades offer you? It must be impressive to make you work so hard at dissuading me."

He withdrew his hand and slapped it against the table. "You're the most stubborn woman I have ever met."

She stood and stared down at him. "I've heard enough." Then she marched out of the café, heavy-hearted with disappointment.

***

Elena stared out the kitchen window, the tamales in front of her untouched. Outside, Gabriella tossed a bone, which Sal limped after. The geraniums Elena had planted had begun to bloom, poking out large, white-tinged pink blossoms among the dark green leaves. Typically all this would cheer Elena, but not today.

Mom glanced over her shoulder while stirring a pot of stew simmering on the range. "What's the matter, *mija*? You haven't touched your plate. Don't you like the tamales?"

"Guess I'm not hungry today." Elena took her fork to a tamale, then hesitated. The thought of food made her stomach turn. Since the moment she left Adam at the café, she'd felt rocks form and settle in her gut. She pushed her plate aside.

Mom closely watched her, concern filling her eyes. She stirred the stew one more time and yelled out the window to Gabby, "Go find Papa. It's time for lunch."

Gabby tossed the stick aside and shot off like a rocket.

Mom took a seat by Elena's side. "What's really bothering you? You can tell your Mama."

Elena half-smiled, but the weight of her pain worked against all efforts to appear more upbeat for her mother's sake. "Really, it's nothing serious. Just a—a minor problem."

Her mother bent and took Elena's face in her hands. Amazing what a mother's touch could do. She felt nurtured and loved in her mother's hands. Even in her misery, she was comforted.

"Tell me."

No use trying to hold anything back, Mom was too attuned to her family for that. "I had an argument with Adam over a work problem. I'm upset about our disagreement, that's all."

Her mother gave her a knowing but loving look. "He means a lot to you, doesn't he? More than you've said."

The urge to cry burned at the back of her throat and she swallowed it down. She nodded.

"I like Adam, too. He's a good man. But his heart belongs to another." Her mother patted her hand. "You must find a man who can love you. One who will also take Gabby into his heart." She sat silent for a moment. Then her eyes lit up. "I have an idea. Silvia Reyes has a son who's about your age, a fine young man. He's a teacher at the community college in Fresno. How about if I find out if he's still available?"

Elena groaned inside. A blind date was the last thing she needed. "You're so sweet, Mom, but I'm not ready to date again."

"Nonsense." Her mother made a clicking sound with her tongue against teeth. "If you're having feelings for Adam, you're ready to meet another man." Her face glowed with possibilities. She looked healthier than she had for some time.

Elena didn't want to burst her bubble. Perhaps her mother was right. A date with Reyes the college professor would take her mind off of Adam. "Okay, Mom, I'll tell you what. Why don't you invite Mr. Reyes— "

"Luis."

"Okay. Why don't you invite Luis Reyes over for dinner so I can meet him?"

Her mother clapped her hands together. "I will." Slowly and stiffly, she rose. "I can't wait to talk to Silvia." Then she hobbled to the ancient wall phone with its long, twisted cord.

***

Three days later, Elena sat across the dinner table from Luis Reyes. Her mother had been successful in setting up a date at the family home, but the dinner was an awkward affair with Elena feeling put on the spot, leaving her little to nothing to say to Luis in front of her family. To fill the silence her mother had taken the lead in questioning him about his life and goals.

Finally, dinner done, her parents excused themselves and took Gabriella and Sal into the house, leaving Elena alone with Luis on the patio. Luis wasn't exactly what Elena had expected. He had to be only a couple inches taller than her, and even though he was handsome in his own way, she found his crooked front teeth distracting. She hated being petty, but the more she saw of him, the less she liked. He had totally ignored Gabby during the meal and given Sal a shove aside with his shiny penny loafers under the table, neither of which helped his cause.

She tried to ignore these thoughts and open herself up to the man beside her. Perhaps he would become more attractive if she gave herself the chance to get to know him better. "Would you like more coffee?"

He held up a hand. "No, *gracias*. I want to sleep tonight. Do you always drink coffee so late?"

She took a sip of the brew. "Always. It's a custom in the Marquez home. An hour without coffee is like a day without sunshine."

"You should know it's not that good for you, all the caffeine. You should be more careful about your health."

Anytime anyone said *should* to her, Elena had the urge to do the opposite. "And what would you suggest?"

He thrust out his chest. "A good diet consists of fruit and vegetables, hardly any sugar or caffeine or alcohol. I try to eat three balanced meals a day and no desserts. And, of course, I drink only purified water. Six to eight glasses a day."

"Of course. And I bet you exercise regularly."

"I jog five miles every morning, come rain or shine. I run my life on a tight schedule. I'm up every day at five, eat a bowl of oatmeal and dry toast, and I'm at school no later than seven-fifteen. Even on weekends and holidays, I keep my mind and body in shape by following this routine."

Elena couldn't help taking another sip of coffee to stay attentive during Luis's account of his regime. "Do you ever vary your schedule?"

"Never. Why would I?"

"For the heck of it?"

He studied her through his lens. "You take your health too lightly. I imagine you're not terribly conscientious about your other habits."

Her hackles rose even higher. "Like what? Keeping my room clean? You're right. I often file my paperwork in piles until I can get to it. I leave my dirty socks in a heap in the corner and I rarely clean out my hairbrush." She probably sounded like a brat, but his controlling attitude made her want to thumb her nose at him.

He simply sat back and considered the cuticle on his manicured nails. She thought about Adam's hands, with his long, slightly calloused fingers. The hands of a man who wasn't afraid to take chances, make a mistake, unlike Luis, whose hands were soft and perfectly groomed.

"You know, Elena, you strike me as a woman who should know better with your education and position."

Was this Luis's slap on the hand with a ruler? She had been judged inadequate. Rather than try to defend herself, Elena shrugged.

Why waste her time and give him the satisfaction? She had lost interest when he toed her dog away, and his negative opinion of her dovetailed nicely into her opinion of him. She had not made his top-ten list of most outstanding women, but he wasn't on hers either. Compared to Adam, Luis wasn't even a distant runner-up. The thought of Adam made her ache anew and all she wanted was to be left alone.

"I don't know about you, Luis, but I have work in the morning. We better call it a night."

He shot out of his seat as though someone had lit a fire beneath him. "Oh, right. I have to be up at—"

"Five o'clock."

"Right."

After a quick goodbye and a wave as Luis headed his compact SUV out of the driveway, Elena wandered back to the house, head full of thoughts about Adam. Rather than help her get over him, this date had confirmed her feelings.

Her mother sat at the kitchen table when she entered the room. "What are you doing up? You're too sick to wait up for me."

Mom's gaze was glued to Elena's face. "Don't worry about me. What happened with Luis? Do you like him?"

As much as she hated to disappoint her mother, Elena had to be truthful. "I'm sure he's an exceptional man, but he's not for me."

Mom's smile drooped. "Why not, *mija*? He's quite good-looking."

"And healthy, but he's kind of...well, he's like a full-time teacher. He was so busy telling me what to do, I would find him hard to be around for long."

"Too bad. I was hoping you two would hit it off and he'd take your mind off of Adam."

Elena bent over and kissed her mother on the forehead. "It's okay, Mom. When I'm ready, I'll find a man on my own."

Her mother levered herself up by using the table. "I know, *mija*. You've always been strong-willed, even at Gabby's age. Why should I expect anything different now?"

Elena laughed. "Sometimes too strong-headed, no?" She took her mother by the arm and walked her toward her room.

Chapter 14

Two days after the disappointing dinner with Luis Reyes, Elena had a follow-up visit with the grieving Lorena. To her surprise, Lorena opened the door with a smile.

"Me much better today," Lorena said hesitantly, trying out her new command of the English language.

The dishes were washed, the furniture dusted, and the table cleared, all indications Lorena was telling the truth. Her hair had been neatly combed back in a ponytail, her shirt was pressed, and her eyes clear.

"Antonio has come and we try to make baby." Lorena blushed and dipped her head. "But I no want what happened again."

Elena placed the tea on the side table. "Me either. I want you to try something for me."

Lorena cocked her head. "*Que?*"

"Where do you get your drinking water?"

When Lorena scrunched up her face, Elena added, "*Agua?*"

"*Si.* At river near Martinez corral."

Exactly what Elena suspected. "I want you to try an experiment. I will provide you with enough money to buy bottled water— *bottelas de agua*—at the general store, but I want you to only drink"—she took a sip of the tea to emphasize her point—"the bottled water, *comprende?*"

"*No.*"

"I think," she tapped her skull, "the *agua es* bad—*mal.* The water may have caused your *problema.*" She patted her stomach to indicate the earlier pregnancy. "Please don't drink the river water."

Lorena's eyes widened while she listened to Elena. "*Si. Yo comprendo.*"

To emphasize her point, Elena pointed at the cup of tea. "Is this from the river water?"

Lorena's mouth dropped open. "Oh, Elena. *Pardon*." She grabbed the cup and emptied its contents outside the door onto the ground.

Relieved she had made herself clear, she fumbled in her purse, pulled out a ten-dollar bill and handed it to Lorena. "Now *compra* only *bottelas de agua*. Tomorrow, I'll arrange to release money for prenatal care so you can purchase purified water during your pregnancy. Promise me that's all you'll drink."

Lorena bobbed her head. "*Si*, Elena. No river *agua. Nada*."

"*Bueno*." Elena moved to the door. "I'll stay in touch to see how you do with the bottled water."

Although buoyed by her hopes for Lorena, Elena left the camp with a nagging sense of loneliness. Lorena had seemed so satisfied in her life now that her grieving had ended and her husband had returned, while Elena felt so out of sync in hers. She missed Adam more than she would have thought possible. She'd known him for a few weeks, and he had a fiancée.

What was wrong with her?

***

All morning Adam had tried repeatedly to complete a brief he needed to file in Sacramento by Tuesday, but he couldn't keep his mind from wandering to thoughts of Elena and their recent encounter. It broke his heart to think she viewed him as the enemy and didn't trust him. While he was committed to representing the power company, he'd never meant to alienate her.

He thought of what he had said to her and cringed. With all her compassion and consideration, his words sounded harsh and unfeeling. She really believed in what she was doing, good or bad, right or wrong. She was like a wild desert bloom in Vandasillo. Without her the town seemed dry and flat.

No matter what Rhoades said, it wouldn't help to stand in her way or discourage her. If she was on the wrong track, she had to discover it for herself, and if not, then Rhoades should be pleased, not fearful of the truth.

In fact, Rhoades said he was certain the plant was in no way responsible for the town's woes, so why be evasive? The quickest way to be free of Elena was to be more helpful. It made Adam wonder what Rhoades was holding back.

***

Between attempts to squeeze tiny letters into minuscule boxes on a government-designed form, Elena picked at a lukewarm enchilada at El Rancho. With only enough time for a quick lunch in town, and no time to file out forms at the office, she had brought her work along to finish at lunch rather than let it cut into family time later. Besides, work kept her mind off of Adam. As she lettered one line, Adam's voice broke through her focused isolation.

"Mind if I join you?"

Her hand slipped and smeared the ink outside the boxes. She jerked her head up and saw him staring down at her, a newspaper tucked under one arm. His contrite grin touched her and she was loath to say no. She nodded while trying to correct her mistake on the form. "Sure. Have a seat."

He moved into the booth opposite her, signaled the waitress, and ordered a *chile relleno* plate.

When they were alone, he turned to her. "I'm glad I bumped into you."

"Why's that?"

He hesitated. "To be truthful, I spotted you through the window and chose to join you. I'm not comfortable with where we left things the other day. I feel like this issue has come between us as friends."

She refused to pick up her fork for fear her hand would tremble and give her away. "I'm not pleased either." She tried to keep her voice modulated. "I was hoping we could keep work and friendship separate, but it's not easy."

He leaned back, studied her face, and seemed to be looking for a clue as to her feelings.

"I'm having one hell of a time being caught between my job defending the plant and my feelings for you and your family."

Elena fiddled with a napkin. "I'm sorry about that, but I don't know how to help you or get around it. I don't like this any better than you do."

He took her free hand in his. "We can overcome this conflict, I'm sure of it."

Elena glanced down at her hand in his, then looked up in time to spot a woman with gray hair in a bun pass the table. Relieved at the diversion, she called, "Good afternoon, Helena," and quickly withdrew her hand.

The woman stopped in front of the table. "Elena, how good to see you. Where have you been keeping yourself?"

"I've been busy working."

Helena looked over at Adam.

"This is my friend, Adam," Elena said, surprised at herself for referring to him as a friend.

Helena bowed her head in his direction. "Elena is my guardian angel. She helped my husband when he first fell ill."

"How's Alonzo?" Elena asked.

"His cancer is in remission and we pray every day it will stay that way."

"I'm so glad. Do send him my best."

Helena squeezed Elena's hand. "I will. But don't let me interrupt your lunch. Have a good meal." She turned and hurried out the door.

"You make quite an impression on people, don't you?" Adam asked.

"I was only doing my job."

He again searched her face, as though looking for something in it.

"Elena, I don't know what I'd do without you…and your family. So far you're my only real friends here in Vandasillo."

She sat silent for a moment. "I wish we didn't have to feud over the power plant, but there's no denying our differences. They seem too vast to bridge."

***

Adam couldn't miss the message. He was stricken. He couldn't imagine going on without her and her family in his life. "We can work things out."

Now it was Elena's turn to reach over and lay a hand on his arm. His skin burned where she touched him, the fire igniting his blood. "Look, you have your agenda and I have mine. There doesn't seem to be a way around the conflict right now." She lowered her lovely eyes and withdrew her hand, the absence of which hurt more than her words. "I think a great deal of you, Adam, but you work for the wrong guys. Until we can get beyond this, we may have to put our friendship on hold."

The waitress placed Adam's plate in front of him and dribbled salsa onto his placemat. "Sorry." She swiped at the placemat with a cloth. "Anything else?"

"Not now." Adam turned his attention back to Elena. "I know what you're saying but you forgot one thing."

"What's that?"

"How important you've become to me. You and your family have been my lifeline in Vandasillo I don't know what I'd have done these last few weeks without you." He stared at her until she flushed and looked away.

"I appreciate your saying that. And you've become important…to my folks and Gabby." Her face flamed hot pink knowing how much he meant to her, too. "But I don't know how we can ignore the elephant between us and go on like it's not there. It's standing in the way of what I need to know about the plant's involvement in poisoning the water, your job to protect them, and whatever friendship has developed between us. As much as I'd like to pretend we can go on as if there aren't major issues between us, I can't."

He gut clenched. "I don't accept that we can't work around it. Maybe I'm being stupid, but I think there has to be a way to remain friends even though we disagree on who's at fault for the problems in this community. You'd think by thirty-four I'd be smart enough to figure a way out of this."

"I don't see how."

Chapter 15

Every seat was occupied in the Fresno medical clinic's waiting room. People were standing against the walls, children played on the floor with Lincoln Logs and Barbie dolls and scrapped with one another over who was in charge. Others discussed their families or their medical conditions. The din caused Elena's head to throb even worse than it had all morning.

A studious-looking young man stood and offered her mother a seat. Elena thanked him profusely since her mother seemed unsteady by her side. She helped her into the seat and handed her the new patient form to fill out.

Her mother took it from her hand. "You look so worried, *mija*. I'm fine. Really I am."

Elena wasn't so certain of that. It had taken Mom an inordinate amount of time to dress that morning and now she appeared weaker than ever. Although Elena made an effort to smile back and reassure her mother, Elena was filled with dread. Two new cases of leukemia had been diagnosed in Vandasillo in the past month and Elena worried there might be a third. She glanced down at Mom. Her shoulders slumped and her head drooped like a turkey's between her shoulder blades, but she kept a courageous smile plastered on her face.

Forty-five minutes later a nurse called for them, and Elena helped her mother into an examination room. Elena helped Mom up onto a white paper-covered exam table in the center of the room and took a chair by the side. A wide counter held various tools: wrapped syringes and glass jars of tongue depressors and gauze pads. Mom glanced around and swallowed hard. "Do you think they'll want my blood?"

"I'm sure they will."

Mom swallowed hard again. "I hope you don't think I'm a chicken, but I've never had anyone take my blood before."

Surprised, Elena wrinkled her nose. "Even when you delivered us?"

"I gave birth to all of you with the help of a midwife. It was no big deal. I've never even been to see a doctor except with you children."

The last person Mom would take care of was herself. Elena's mother had always sacrificed her own needs in service to her family. This had to be difficult for her: giving up being the caretaker and accepting being taken care of.

Of course, Elena chuckled to herself. A pinecone doesn't fall far from the tree. She could have been describing herself, except her family extended to the community. "It's not bad, Mom, if you look the other way. Don't watch when they stick the needle in and you'll hardly notice more than a minor prick."

"And I've dealt with a few of those in my time." Mom's cheeks turned bright crimson.

Elena laughed, but she couldn't help wondering if Mom had Ron in mind. Funny, she hadn't thought much about Ron in the last couple weeks, a shift explainable by Adam's growing presence in her life.

A tall, big-boned woman entered the room carrying a clipboard. She had the shoulder span of a man, and large, prominent features. When she smiled, she had a warmth that lit up the room and immediately put Elena at ease.

"*Hola.* I'm Doctor Gonzales." She reached out and shook Mom's hand. "You must be Frieda Marquez."

"*Si.* And this is my daughter, Elena."

Dr. Gonzales acknowledged her.

"We were expecting Dr. Keating," Elena said.

Dr. Gonzales studied the clipboard. "I've recently joined Dr. Keating in this practice because he's gotten so busy. I hope you don't mind me examining your mother."

Just the opposite. Elena was relieved to have this warm woman working with her mother rather than Dr. Keating with his usual cocky attitude. "Not at all. We only want to find out why she is so weak and tired all the time. It's not like her."

"You exaggerate, *mija.* Not all the time." She dipped her head. "But some of the time."

104

Dr. Gonzales turned to Elena. "Would you mind stepping out of the room while I examine your mother? You can wait outside the door. When I'm finished, I'll call you back in."

"No problem." Elena did as she was asked and found a seat in the hall. Two nurses scurried past in starched white uniforms going in opposite directions. The one about to enter her mother's room asked, "Would you like a magazine?"

When Elena nodded the nurse brought a handful of choices. She flipped through the pages, barely able to concentrate on stories. After she had skimmed half the magazines, Dr. Gonzales extended her head out the doorway.

"Would you like to rejoin us?"

Elena's pulse pounded as she reentered the room. "How is she?"

"On first glance, I can't find anything terribly wrong with your mother, except for the symptoms you describe. Her lungs are clear, the heart's strong and steady as a drum, and blood pressure's in the normal range. My only concern is her swollen glands. We drew blood and I took a pap smear."

Her mother flashed her arm at Elena. A white slash of bandage covered the inside of her elbow like a white badge of courage. "It hardly hurt."

"How long until we know something, Doctor?" Elena asked.

"Up to a week for the labs. If there's anything that shows up, you will hear from us immediately. If not, count your blessings. Your mother may have a minor infection that will clear up on its own."

"Let's hope." Doubt nagged beneath Elena's optimism.

***

The brown manila envelope with a return label from the lab where Elena sent the water sample lay on her desk. Her hand shook when she lifted it. Inside this plain-wrapped package was the answer to one of her most pressing questions, and, perhaps, the future of her community, never mind her friendship with Adam.

She had to gather up the nerve to open it.

Primed with two deep breaths, she tore open the top of the envelope and extracted the report. The laboratory had sent back a two-page written summary along with two pages of data in neatly labeled columns. She reviewed the report twice, not believing her eyes. The figures varied widely from those collected by the power plant.

As soon as she calmed the flutter in her chest, she picked up the phone and dialed Adam's office. His answering service said he was out but would return her call.

Elena reread the report in case she had made a mistake the first time through. The data remained unchanged. She sat back and tried to process that the power company had fudged their findings by submitting a sample sourced elsewhere or by arranging for a bogus analysis. What had previously been passing speculation asserted itself irrefutably in the printed report before her. The hubris of the perpetrators stunned her.

While waiting for Adam's return call, she made copies of the report, an extra one for her file and one for Adam. She looked up from the copy machine as Maria Ortega entered the office. Maria's full face was flush from the sun.

"Elena, I have been meaning to stop by and see you."

Elena made her way to where Maria stood and gave her a hug. "Good to see you. How have you been?"

Maria scrunched up her full face and raised her shoulders. "How do you think? I am recovering."

"I'm glad. Have a seat." Maria gingerly lowered herself into the chair across from her. Elena pointed to the phone. "I'm expecting an important call and will have to take it if it comes in."

Maria raised a hand. "*No problema.* I only have a moment. Pedro's at the feed store for barley." Maria's mood turned somber. "I stopped by to tell you about Carmen Villa. You know she's my neighbor?"

"What happened?"

"She died from the blood disease yesterday."

Elena felt a stab of icy fear in her stomach. "How awful."

"She had been too weak, could hardly stand. A mere cold killed her." Maria's frown deepened and, for the first time, Elena noticed her eyes were puffy.

With the verdict still out on her mother's health, this news disturbed Elena more than it normally would. "I'm so sorry to hear that. Doesn't she have one son at home?"

"Gregorio is seventeen. Pedro and I plan to take him in to live with us until he's out of school. We were wondering if you had a way to help us with him?"

"Of course. I'll let you know when I've arranged something."

The phone's ring interrupted her. She put the receiver to her ear and heard Adam's deep, resonant voice. "Hold on one moment, Adam. I have a client." She covered the speaker with her palm and said to Maria, "This is the call I mentioned. I'll stop by your home tomorrow at," she perused her schedule book, "two to meet with you and Pedro."

Maria rose and backed toward the door. "*Muchas gracias*," she said as she made her way out.

Elena uncovered the phone. "Sorry to keep you waiting."

"What's up?" Adam asked.

"I received water analysis report from the lab and I want to show it to you."

"And?"

"I really don't want to discuss it on the phone. Could we set a time to meet at your office?"

He made a sound as though blowing air through his teeth. "This is all pretty mysterious, Elena. You're not going to keep me in suspense, are you?"

"It won't be for long if you have time today."

"Then I'll make the time. Hold on." She heard his muffled voice tell his secretary he'd be with her in a moment. "It's a busy day, but let's say after five. I'll keep the time open."

"I'll be there."

***

Elena extended a copy of the report across the desk. She watched as Adam scanned it, then puffed out his bottom lip. She had to press her advantage. "As you can see"—she pointed toward the papers in his hand—"this is a far cry from the power plant's report."

He blew out a burst of air. "I'd say."

"Look at the data on the toxins. According to the lab, the concentration is well above safe drinking levels. They're actually in the dangerous zone."

Adam lowered the report to the desktop and held her eyes. "Of course, this report raises more questions than it answers."

"Like what?"

"Like the obvious one. Why the huge discrepancy between the power company's reports and yours? And, if your report's accurate, where is the pollution coming from? All that is still unclear."

Elena sat perfectly still except for the hands knitting invisible yarn in her lap. She felt herself losing ground and needed to make her point. "But these numbers are irrefutable."

"So are the power company's. As a matter of fact, they have two similar results to yours and they have taken theirs under pristine conditions, with full scientific protocol. Can you say the same?"

If he considered a Ball jar scientific instrumentation and Herman's surveillance professional observation. "But—"

"But what? You know as well as I do, they have more valid measures at the moment."

She wanted to debate him, but it seemed futile. "They have more of a vested interest in the outcome."

"And you don't?" As though to punctuate his point, he leaned back in his chair and placed his hands behind head. A slight five o'clock shadow speckled his strong jaw and light circles were etched under his eyes. This job wore him down more than she realized—or was it something else? She wished she could reach over and caress his cheek, run fingers through his thick, shiny hair to comfort him, but she had long learned to rein in errant affection.

"Okay. Let's look at this from a legal point of view. Say you were to take on the role of an impartial judge and I presented you with both these pieces of information. What would you think?"

"But I took the sample from a—"

"Step out of yourself. You're no longer Elena Marquez the social worker. You're Elena Marquez, judge and jury. Your job is to fairly and impartially evaluate the evidence and come to a conclusion concerning the data. On one hand, you have a social worker with a single report that appears to show the ground water's polluted. On the other hand, a major power company has two reports saying the same water isn't in the least contaminated. Who would you believe?"

Elena bobbed her head in thought. "I see your point even though I can't agree with it."

"And even if your report is totally accurate, you have no valid proof the power company's polluting the groundwater. As a judge, I'd be hard-pressed to find them at fault."

Elena stared past Adam at a grouping of his diplomas on the wall behind him. "I have an idea that will at least address the first of your concerns."

"Go ahead."

"What if you were to join me in collecting a second water sample from one of the local fields? We could send it in to the lab together. Then you'd be a witness to the source of the sample and the collection methods."

He raised both hands, palms forward. "I don't doubt your sample."

"Granted, but you doubt the accuracy of the sample. I think it would be useful for you to see where, when, and how it's collected and sent. That might quiet one of the questions. If the results are the same as these," she pointed at the report on his desk, "then we'll decide together where to go from there. What do you say?"

He thought about it a long moment, too long in her estimation. She was preparing herself for the struggle when he said, "I can do that. It won't take too much time away from my other commitments and I can serve as the company's eyes and ears to see if the process is done correctly. When do you want to meet?"

Chapter 16

Flat fields extended in every direction as far as Adam could see, occasionally interrupted by a road, or by a silo, or a barn. Elena had taken the lead and he trailed her through peppers and squash plants, past workers in ragged khakis and tees with floppy hats and bandanas around their foreheads, to a babbling brook.

She stood and waited for him to catch up to her. When he did, she gestured at the brook. "This water irrigates the fields along this road. All four people recently diagnosed with leukemia worked these fields on and off over the past year. I thought this might be as good a place as any to take the sample. Did you bring a sanitized Ball jar?"

He went into his pack and extracted the jar. The night before he had boiled water for fifteen minutes and then submerged the jar in it. He had been careful not to touch the jar with his hands and had immediately capped it once it was out of the water. "Here." He handed it to her.

She tore open a packet of plastic kitchen gloves and covered her hands before unscrewing the jar's cap. He watched while she submerged the jar in the water and when it was half full she took it out and replaced the top, handing it to him. "It's in your hands."

They walked together back to their cars where she opened her passenger-side door and took out a labeled box. "It's ready for you to submit. All you have to do is seal and send."

He took the box from her and tossed it into the open window of the Jeep. "You'll call me as soon as you have the results?"

"Don't worry about it. You'll be the first to hear."

He patted the daypack. "I'll send it off on my way to Los Angeles. I have business there." He glanced at his watch. "I better get going. Have a great weekend."

"You too." The look in her eyes was wrenching. He had to tear himself away.

***

Once Adam's car was no longer in view, the tears she had held back dribbled down her face. She knew what kind of business he had in Los Angeles and it hurt her heart to consider it. She slid into the driver's seat and drove to a spot she knew well, a spot where she often went to let out her misery in private. Under an old cottonwood tree, its branches shading the relentless sun, she stepped from the car and sat on a partially exposed root. With her head lowered into her hands, she released the remainder of the tears which had been burning at the back of her throat. Once the storm had passed, she sat quietly, contemplating her emotions.

She could no longer deceive herself into believing her feelings for Adam were professional and platonic, not after her reaction today. The thought of him in the arms of another woman was more than she could bear. She considered moving away from Vandasillo, but she could never leave her mother at a time like this. She didn't know what to do, but before she made any decisions, she would have to get a handle on herself.

She wiped her wet cheeks with the back of her hand and foraged about in her purse for a scrap of tissue. Finding none, she turned her face to the sun and let it dry her eyes. She had always prided herself on her strength and resiliency in the face of adversity or frustration. This situation was no different than any other. She would find the inner fortitude to overcome her ridiculous and ill-founded feelings for Adam. Even if she had to steel herself against him and keep her walls fortified, she would not allow him to affect her this way again. She had priorities in her life, as he had in his, and hers included her work and her family. From now on, he would only be a distant friend and colleague, no different from any other. She would exile him from her heart forever.

***

"Take a seat, Adam." Douglass Lubbock motioned Adam toward a chair across the desk from him. For a partner in a prominent LA law firm, Lubbock's appearance contradicted his status. He could be any man on any construction site downtown with his ruddy complexion and slicked-back red hair. Broad cheeks and dark underarm stains on his white shirt rounded out the impression. "I'm glad you could make the meeting today."

Adam took the seat and waited anxiously to hear what would motivate Lubbock to ask him to drop everything and rush back to Los Angeles. "You said it was important, so I made a point of being here."

Lubbock cleared his throat. "Before we start, I wanted to say how sorry I am to hear about your broken engagement with Brittany Budman. Cyrus told me about it yesterday. It's too bad things didn't work out for you two."

Adam swallowed. He had anticipated the breakup might become an issue in the office, but he didn't think it would be so soon. And he hoped it didn't put him on shaky ground with the firm because he was the most recent hire.

Lubbock plied a finger under his collar. "And sorry for the short notice, but I received a call from Rhoades yesterday. I don't know how to tell you this."

His hesitation made Adam shift forward in his seat. "Yes?"

Before Lubbock could answer, his phone rang.

"What? Tell him I'll call him back as soon as I'm finished here. And Betty, hold the rest of my calls." He hung up. "Where was I? Oh yes, Rhoades is unhappy with the job you're doing in Vandasillo. He feels you're not adequately representing the power company's position."

Adam's pulse pounded in his head. The last thing he wanted to do was lose this client. It would be professional suicide. He took a studied breath. "I have a tough situation in Vandasillo. I know my job is to represent the power plant, but there's growing evidence that run-off from the plant may be at the root of the community's medical problems. It's hard to contradict the facts."

Lubbock shook his head. "That's not what Rhoades tells me. He says he has substantiated evidence that the power plant is not at fault." Lubbock picked up a sheaf of obviously faxed paper. "He's even faxed me independent testing to prove his point." Lubbock studied the sheaf. "Rhoades seems to believe a certain local social worker with a personal vendetta has blurred your vision."

Adam's vision went red for a moment and he wanted to scream. He had to tamp down the anger that rose in him before he could speak. "Look, that certain social worker you mentioned has a conflicting report that shows the water near the power plant is contaminated with cancer-causing chemicals. It's difficult to refute her evidence."

Lubbock narrowed his eyes and leaned across his desk, his barrel-like chest grazing the top. "But refute her you must. Your job is to do your best to exonerate the power plant of all charges of wrongdoing. You aren't being paid to listen to some crackpot social worker's tear-jerking, blubbering campaign against the company. You're being paid to prove her wrong and to protect a major service company that provides electricity and gas to a large area of inland California. This company, I might remind you, is more valuable to the people in Vandasillo than that social worker, any day."

"But I'm not certain she's mistaken."

"We at Goodman, Lubbock, Weinrab and Budman have no desire to place you, or any of our staff, in a position where you feel compromised. If you're not up to the job in Vandasillo, we have already recruited another lawyer, Bob Herman, to step in. He's expressed interest in taking on the challenge."

Adam cringed inside. Bob was the last person he wanted to lose his position to. Bob had already been assigned the Armand case over Adam. He was the rising star of the freshmen attorneys. Adam had no desire to further Bob's vaulting ambitions, especially if it required slitting his own throat. He held up a hand. He wouldn't allow Lubbock to replace him without a fight. Besides the blow to his career, it would mean never working with Elena again. She'd most certainly end up a casualty. The thought turned his stomach. "I can do it."

"What? I can hardly hear you. Speak up, man." Lubbock slapped a hand on the desk in an obvious power play.

"I said that I want a chance to complete what I began. I can do the job, contrary to what Rhoades believes."

Lubbock eyed him, then sighed. "All right, but if I hear one more complaint from Rhoades about your performance, you better start packing your office. Understand?"

Adam rose, more than ready to leave the room and Lubbock's penetrating stare. "You couldn't be clearer. I'll do my job for the firm as I always have, to the best of my ability."

Lubbock stood and faced him, a small smile creasing the corners of his thin lips. "That's the spirit, my man. We want to see you succeed. Now go back to Vandasillo and represent all of us here at Goodman, Lubbock, Weinrab and Budman."

"I will." Adam fled the room and made it down the hall to the inside of the men's room before he slumped against the stall's closed door, a hand to his middle. The enormity of his dilemma tied his churning gut into a knot. If he did what Lubbock wanted, no matter the facts, he'd lose Elena forever. And if Elena's assertions were proven true, he'd have to sell out his own integrity and deny the truth to fulfill his job. But if he stood by Elena he might as well toss his career with Goodman, Lubbock, Weinrab and Budman—or for that matter any of the large California defense firms—down the commode in front of him, and let it flush away his dreams.

***

"Adam, I thought you would still be in Los Angeles." Elena nervously ran a hand through her hair. She hadn't expected company, especially Adam, and was not prepared to see him. She glanced down at her torn jeans and tie-dyed shirt, embarrassed. She looked up to see the stricken look in his eyes and her self-consciousness immediately vanished. "Is everything all right?"

He waved a hand in front of her face. "Fine. Fine. I've been worried about your mother. How is she?"

"Who's that?" Mom's weak voice came from the living room.

"Adam, Mom. He's come to see how you're doing."

Her mother's voice brightened. "How nice. Invite him in."

"Nah, I think I'll leave him out to dry." Elena offered Adam a conspiratorial smile. "Come on in."

Adam trailed her into the living room where her mother sat propped on pillows with Sal at her feet, looking as serene as a monk in meditation. As soon as she saw Adam, she reached out her hand and took his. Sal wagged his tail but didn't rise. "Adam, I'm so pleased you stopped by."

He withdrew his hand from behind his back and presented her with a bouquet of mixed flowers. "Thought these might make you feel better." He held them out to her. She grasped them and gushed, "Oh, they're beautiful."

He looked as pleased as Mom.

"I better find a vase." In the kitchen Elena spotted a vase stuck high on a shelf above the sink. She climbed on a chair and brought it down, pausing to fill it halfway with tap water. Back in the living room, she placed the flowers in the vase and put it on the coffee table in front of her mother.

Mom ran her fingertips over blossoms. "You are so thoughtful, Adam. *Muchas gracias*." She was the most animated Elena had seen her in weeks and it raised her hopes, if only for a moment.

"Mom, don't overdo it. I'm sure Adam will understand if you have to rest."

Elena sent Adam a look and he immediately said, "Of course, I didn't mean to disturb you. I wanted to see how you were feeling."

Mom looked at Elena sideways. "My daughter is too protective of me. She thinks it's my nap time. I'll only agree to rest on one condition: Adam stays for dinner." She turned to him. "Elena has cooked up a wonderful chili stew."

Even though Elena wasn't sure being around Adam alone would be good for her, she wanted to please her mother. Adam's presence seemed to cheer her.

"I'd love to stay, but only if you let me do a bit of the work around here."

She placed a finger over her lips in contemplation. "The evenings are getting colder. We could use more kindling for the porch fireplace."

"Then I'm the man for the job," he said. "All I'll need is a woodpile and an axe."

"I think we can accommodate you." Elena took him around the side of the house to a large pyramid-shaped stack of wood. Leaning against the pile was a long-handled red axe. "Your instrument of torture."

"Torture to whom?"

Me, she thought, but said, "You, of course. Chopping wood is my least favorite task around here. I'd almost rather clean out the septic tank."

His eyes opened wide in mock horror. "Really?"

"Nah, but chopping wood's a close second."

"You've never seen a master at work."

She stood back and watched Adam withdraw a log, stand it on its end, raise the axe and split the log in two with one swift swing.

When he raised the axe again, she noticed how his shirt accentuated his broad chest and strong arms.

After cleaving four large logs, Adam drew a deep breath and wiped perspiration from his brow. "Whew. It's hotter than I thought. Hope you don't mind me taking off my shirt."

"You do have an advantage over me. I can't remove mine."

A cockeyed smile lit up his face. "Sure, you can."

She laughed. "Right."

"I wouldn't tell." He unbuttoned his shirt and folded it over a tree stump. "So how's she doing, for real?"

She tried not to stare at his sinewy back. "About the same. We're still waiting to hear from the doctor."

When he turned around, she couldn't take her eyes off his muscular chest covered with a generous sprinkling of brown hair. She cleared her throat to chase away the overwhelming desire that lodged itself there. "You look like you've been at this for years."

"I'm not exactly ready for the iron man contest, especially after sitting for hours at a desk job."

"Could have fooled me." She forced herself to stop staring and looked away, but a funny feeling continued to swirl in the pit of her stomach. "Better finish chopping. I need to stir the stew soon."

When she glanced back up, he'd moved so close it took her breath away. She met his eyes, and the passion in his set her aflame. Before she had a chance to step aside, he leaned forward and pressed his lips against hers.

The flames burst free inside her and the firestorm ignited every single cell in her body. When he wrapped her in his arms and drew her to him, the feel of his warm, naked flesh against her fingers, the light scent of his aftershave, the taste of his rich, strong tongue in her mouth was almost more than she could bear. Helpless to restrain herself, she leaned into him allowing him to deepen his embrace. The kiss lasted what seemed like an hour and made time stand still. In the work of a moment, everything in the universe changed.

When she came up for air, his breathing was ragged, his face flushed. She wanted him more than she ever thought possible, far more than she had ever wanted anyone else before, even her ex. But this man was forbidden fruit and would take her to a poisonous place, a place of compromise, betrayal and abandonment. She would never go there and betray herself, her work or another woman.

Abruptly, she pushed him away with palms on his chest. "I'm...sorry. I don't know what came over me. We shouldn't have done that."

Passion still shone in his eyes, tinted his cheeks. "Yes, we should have."

Her head had cleared enough to make sense of what had gone on and she didn't like it one bit. While her desire for him was natural, the last thing he should be doing was making a pass at her. The man had a fiancée, for God's sake. Since he seemed totally unrepentant for his actions, her respect for him lessened. "Look, I like you as a friend, but I'm not interested in anything more serious. Right now we need to keep our relationship professional. We both have too much at stake here to allow anything to deter us from our goal. Besides, you're already taken."

"But..."

Adam at a loss for words? Amazing. "We either keep a professional distance or we go back to meeting solely at the office and speak only about the power company and the community. I don't want anything to affect our professional duties. I appreciate your concern for my mother, but I will have to ask you not to come around if this goes any further."

"Momma. Adam." Gabby ran up to them, panting heavily. Thank heaven for her adorable daughter. She had saved the day.

"Is dinner ready yet?" Gabby asked.

"In a moment. Why don't you go in and wash up?" When Gabriella ran off, Elena turned her attention back to Adam. "As you hear, I have to go."

He shuffled his feet and studied the ground. "I didn't mean to offend you. I've come to really like you a lot."

She drew back, unable to look at him. She liked him too, too much, but this was inappropriate. "Maybe it would be best if we forget dinner tonight, I think it would be awkward. I'll make up an excuse for you. Let's try to keep this purely professional from now on."

He toyed with the axe handle. "I'm not going anywhere until I finish chopping wood."

He would play with her the same way he did with the axe and then toss her to the side like the logs when he was done and ready to go back to his woman in Los Angeles. "That's your choice. If you do, please leave the kindling over there." She pointed to a slab by the patio. "I have to check on the stew." Before she could change her mind and invite him into her house and her life, she scurried away to the safety of the kitchen. Tears welled up in her eyes and she choked them back. She couldn't let him or the family see her pain.

As soon as she reached the kitchen she closed the door behind her and slumped into a chair. When she thought she was safe, she released the sobs still trying to escape. She had never felt so torn in her life. A big part of her desperately wanted this man and would have given everything, her heart, her soul, her life, to be with him, but a saner part knew she could never give herself to a man she couldn't trust. A man who would use her to advance his own agenda. A man who would be unfaithful: a man from a world alien to hers who would eventually return to his predetermined life, and leave her behind.

Besides, she had Gabriella to think about. Gabby had already sustained the loss of one important man in her short life. Elena couldn't allow her to undergo the loss of another. It would leave her with perpetual anxiety around men that could affect the remainder of her years. Elena couldn't countenance the thought.

Ron had left her with more than a broken heart. He had left her with a legacy of fear. But fear made you smart. She would never again open herself up to someone who spelled trouble, no matter how much she craved him. And she would never want to harm another woman, no matter the sacrifice.

***

That kiss confirmed what he'd suspected for some time now: he hungered for Elena. Adam had subverted his desire and his need in order to fulfill his obligation to Brittany. But now he was free and he couldn't get Elena out of his mind. No matter how hard he tried, and he did try, he would have done almost anything to eliminate the longing that had taken hold of him and was driving him crazy. He could think of little else.

Yet, he hadn't told her the truth about the breakup with Brittany. The only answer that made sense was how embarrassed he was by the way he had been played as a fool. When Elena had pushed him away, his first inclination was to believe she didn't want him either, a by-product of being so recently scorned. Since he had yet to overcome the blow to his ego and the subsequent humiliation, it was easy to interpret Elena's reaction as further proof he was undesirable. But it was possible she was merely protecting herself from someone she still believed to be engaged to another woman.

The only way to find out was to tell her the truth and watch for her reaction.

He drove back to his office and tried to concentrate on filling out paperwork Rhoades had sent him the day before, but every time he started to write, his mind wandered and he would lose track of what he was doing and find himself thinking of Elena. He was besotted and bewitched. That his feelings might be unrequited was one of two huge problems. She was the enemy. If he was with her, he'd have to leave the firm and start over who knew where.

Unable to complete anything, he left the office and headed home. Perhaps the nightly news would take his mind off his preoccupation. He flicked on the TV, but his thoughts were of Elena. He turned off the TV and went for a walk.

The wind had picked up and blew dust in his face. He ignored the grit in his hair, his nose, his mouth, and walked on. Before long he found himself in front of Elena's office. And then he knew what he had to do. He had to prove to her he was worthy of her affection, her love. He could, he would, find a way into her heart.

Chapter 17

"I called to apologize for yesterday. I didn't mean to offend you."
Elena took a deep breath in anticipation of Adam's response. She
wanted to put space between them but couldn't afford to alienate
him. She had taken time to consider, and she still needed him too
much.

A long pause at the other end of the line made her heart flutter,
and pounding filled her head. Her fingers quivered against the
receiver.

"I wasn't expecting to hear from you this soon."

Did he sound distant or was it only her imagination playing
tricks on her? "My mother was disappointed when you weren't at
dinner. I felt so guilty. I probably overreacted."

He cleared his throat. "So your mother put you up to this?"

"No. Well, I mean, she wanted me to speak with you, but this
was my idea. I don't feel good about the way I dealt with things."
She paused, remembering the kiss. A tingle traveled up her spine and
heat came up her neck to her cheeks. She called because she could
think of nothing else since they parted. She could hardly breathe at
the thought she might never be with him again, that she might lose
him as a friend. She couldn't conceive of life without him even if she
couldn't be with him in the way she truly wanted. "I heard from the
clinic. My mother's hematocrit...you know, her red blood count...is
off. They're concerned enough to want to see her again tomorrow."

"What time?"

"Three in the afternoon."

"I have to reschedule an appointment, but I'll be there."

If she had been in his presence, she'd have given him a huge
hug. "I didn't call to induce you into coming along, but I thought
you'd like to know her status. Thanks for the offer, but I'll be fine
taking her to the clinic myself."

"This isn't about you. I want to be there for her."

Elena couldn't suppress the smile that tugged at her lips. In his own way, he was always there for her and her family. "Meet me at the house at two."

"See you there. And Elena..."

Her pulse raced. "Yes?"

"I accept your apology."

***

Dr. Gonzales was at the desk taking a phone call when she motioned Adam and Elena to seats across from her. When she hung up, she made a notation on a pad. "Sorry. It's always busy around here." She tore the paper off the pad and stuck it in an appointment book. "I wanted to speak to you while your mother dressed."

Elena sat forward, her face drawn, stress lines etched around her mouth and eyes. "What's going on?"

"As I said on the phone, we're concerned about your mother's hematocrit. With an increase in the number of small lymphocytes in the blood, we have to rule out leukemia as a possibility."

Elena blanched and white-knuckled the desk. The doctor watched her. "Sorry to be so abrupt."

Adam was torn between wanting to comfort Elena and wanting to learn the truth. "How do you make a differential diagnosis?"

"We drew more blood for a detailed and specific set of tests. If that fails, we have to take bone marrow, but usually the blood tells the story. It should give us a better understanding of what's happening in your mother's body. We should have the results in three or four days. I will call you personally as soon as I know something."

A call from the doctor directly was serious business. "What will it mean for Frieda if she's diagnosed with leukemia?" He asked.

"The course of treatment depends on the type of leukemia." Dr. Gonzales turned to Elena. "I want you to know with the new treatments available, leukemia is often quite manageable, and people can live for years in remission. I don't want you to see this diagnosis as a death sentence."

Elena stared at the doctor, wringing her hands. How much she had absorbed wasn't clear. He figured he'd have to go over it with her again later.

"With proper treatment, at least one complete and extended remission can be induced in all patients," the doctor continued. "As many as three successive complete remissions are not unusual. If your mother has leukemia, she may live as long as she would have without it. Of course, there's no guarantee, but it's not uncommon."

He placed a hand around Elena's upper arm, noting he could easily reach around and touch fingertips and gave it a squeeze. She nodded at him then looked at the doctor. "Thank you for telling me that. It's a relief to know she has a chance."

A knock at the door distracted them.

"Come in," Dr. Gonzales said.

A nurse poked her head into the room and brushed fiery red hair, too red to be real, off her face. "The patient's dressed and ready."

"We shouldn't keep her waiting in her condition." Dr. Gonzales rose. "Any more questions at this time?"

Elena shook her head. "Maybe later."

In the waiting room, Frieda leaned against a ledge, her knees wobbly. Adam rushed up and took her by the arm. "Let's take you home." He escorted her to Elena's car.

When they were out of earshot, Frieda leaned into him and whispered, "What did the doctor say?"

He exchanged glances with Elena and her eyes told him to answer. She seemed relieved it would be him to say the words to her mother. "They need more tests to see what's happening inside you. You must be keeping a secret."

Frieda stumbled then righted herself with his help. "If you saw what's in here," she thumped on her chest, "you'd keep it a secret, too."

His laugh disguised the anxiety lurking below the surface.

"The doc says you're going to outlive us all, Mom, but I could have told her that." Elena held the car door open for her.

"Not with the way I've been feeling lately, *mija*," Frieda said as she ducked into the car.

Gabby and Sal rushed the car as soon as they drove onto the property. Before they came to a full stop, Gabby had grabbed a hold of the driver's side handle, her head by the open window. He felt Elena swerve slightly to avoid drifting into her.

"Be careful."

When the car stopped, Gabby opened Elena's door. "How's Nana?"

"Okay. Where your Grandpa?"

Gabby clung to her. "In the field."

While Elena walked Gabby to the house, Adam helped Frieda limp alongside him then settled her on the sofa.

"Thanks, Adam. I don't know what we'd do without you," Elena said, the look of gratitude in her eyes reinforcing her words.

"No *problema*. That's why I'm here."

Frieda looked pastier than ever. "That trip beat me up. Would you all mind if I went to lie down in my bed for a few minutes?"

"I'll go with you, Nana," Gabriella said.

"No, *mi nièta*, you go play." Frieda struggled to rise.

Deep lines encircled Elena's mouth. "Do you want me to help you, Mom?"

"I'll be fine." Frieda pushed herself to her feet and stumbled to her room then closed the door behind her.

Elena's gaze met his and he felt helpless. He wanted to take her in his arms and protect her, but instead he told her, "Don't worry. You're doing everything you can."

The dubious look that came over her face told him she didn't believe him.

"Gabby, would you mind going to fetch your grandpa? I'm sure he'd like to know how Nana's doing."

"Sure, Mama." Gabby left the room with Sal panting at her feet.

After she was gone, Elena stared out the window and watched her cross the yard. "Gabriella suspects that there's a problem. She's not her spunky self."

He came up behind her and watched the long-legged girl until she disappeared from sight. "What have you told her?"

Elena turned and, for a moment, his breath caught. Her eyes were luminous with tears that threatened to spill at any moment. "That Nana is sick, but she senses the severity of the illness. I hadn't realized what a sensitive person she's become. She was always so rambunctious, I never saw the hurt inside her."

"Children can cope with a lot." He stared past her, remembering his parents' raised voices, and the ugly scenes.

"But she's coped with too much already." With those words, the tears overflowed and tumbled down her cheeks.

To comfort her, he drew her into his arms and allowed her to release her tears against his chest. Holding her close, he could feel the softness of her skin, smell the heavenly scent of her hair while he heard the anguish of her tears. He wanted to ally her pain, vanquish her fear, make her whole and healed. "It's all right," he whispered into her ear while stroking her back.

He held her until she stopped crying, then he stepped back and looked into her eyes. The spark that had never died caught fire again and flamed inside him. Before he could consider the consequences or question what he was doing, he lowered his lips onto hers and kissed her. Even as he touched his lips to hers, he tasted the tantalizing bittersweet taste of her mouth, listened to the ragged rasp of her breath, he knew he cherished her above all else and always would.

To his surprise, instead of pulling back, she responded with fervor and allowed him to kiss her as the fire raged inside him. When he hoped this would go on forever, she suddenly jerked away.

"I'm sorry. I'm vulnerable right now. Please don't hold this against me. We shouldn't be doing this. You're engaged to someone else. It's not right."

The reckoning had been postponed for far too long. The time had arrived to come clean. He took a deep breath. "I'm no longer engaged. I broke it off a few weeks ago."

She poked a finger into his chest with more force than was necessary. "Why didn't you say something sooner?"

"I didn't know what to say. I felt stupid about the whole thing. I made a dumb mistake and I wasn't ready to let anyone know about it."

She turned her head to stare out the window. He couldn't tell whether she was angry or relieved.

"I'm sorry that happened to you, but it's still wrong for us to be acting this way. We have our jobs to do. We need to stay impartial, at least until we sort this water situation out." She glanced out at the sun porch. "Gabby will be back in a second with my dad," she said in a breathless voice, combing her fingers through hair. "I need to spend time with her alone. I'd better make coffee first."

***

Herman Molar paced Elena's office, impatiently waiting for her to end her telephone call. Every now and then he would stop in front of her desk and listen to her end of the conversation, then begin pacing again. His nervous energy seared through the room and prompted her to speed up the call.

When she said goodbye and placed the receiver down, he stood before her. "Well?"

She suppressed a smile at his childlike excitement. "You have a new job starting tomorrow at eight. It's at the Cleary farm. Here's the address and directions." She jotted the information down on a sticky note. Herman's unemployment insurance was barely enough to cover his living expenses and he had come in begging for her help. The Cleary farm had been her first thought. She handed Herman the note.

He glanced at it and then up at her. "What will I do on a farm?"

"You'll be overseeing the packing of crates to be shipped to market. The Cleary farm is a busy one. You'll have plenty to keep you occupied."

He shook his head of limp brown hair, which hung down below his slightly protruding ears. "Elena, yuse a doll. Yuse really is. I can't tell yuse how much this means to me."

"This is part of my job. Besides, I owe you one."

Herman whistled. "Yuse got that one right."

She rose and walked to the window. She stared out at the late afternoon traffic and watched as Serena entered the general store. Down the street, another client, Jesus, left the barbershop. She kept her back to Herman. "There is one thing you could do for me."

"What's that?"

"If you know of anything going on at the plant that might have a bearing on the number of recent cancer cases and birth defects in this community, I'd like to know." She turned to face him.

His unflinching gaze met hers. "I'd owe yuse that one, but I don't know nothin' that would help yuse out. I swear."

Disappointed, Elena stopped long enough to take a deep breath before continuing. "If you remember anything, even if it seems insignificant to you, I want to know."

Herman stuck the note in his gray pants pocket and began to move to the door. "Sure. Sure. No problem. If I tink of anything, yuse be the first to know. Thanks again." He was out the door before she could say more, leaving his unfulfilled promise behind, a promise that may never be satisfied.

Elena went back to her desk and withdrew a file from one of her piles, determined to catch up on her charting before her next client. In mid-sentence, the phone rang. She picked it up.

Her mother's voice sounded strained. "Elena, you better come home."

She froze. "What's the matter? Are you ill? Is it Gabby? Dad?"

"No, no, *mija*. I didn't mean to worry you. Everyone is fine here. You have a visitor."

Perplexed, Elena pulled the phone closer to her ear. "I wasn't expecting anyone."

"Neither was I, and I have to entertain him until you come home," her mother whispered. "I'm getting awfully tired."

"Why are you being so mysterious? Who is it?"

A silence filled the phone, then Frieda sighed. "Ronald's here."

***

By the kitchen door, Elena looked past Frieda to see Ron standing by the sink. His dirty blond hair had been neatly cut and he wore a pair of charcoal chinos and a white knit short-sleeved shirt. He looked young and innocent, even boyish. A smile plastered his lips.

Moving toward her, he held out a bouquet of daisies. "It's good to see you." When her mother stepped aside, he pressed the daisies into her shaking hand.

The last thing in the world she wanted right now was to deal with Ron. "What are you doing here?"

He ducked his head demurely. "I know you weren't expecting me, but I wanted to see Gabriella." He looked up with a hopeful expression. "And you."

"Well, you've seen us. Is that all you want?"

The look on her mother's face could have stopped a semi, but she ignored the shocked expression. "I hate to be rude, but we aren't prepared to entertain you."

He frowned. "I don't want entertainment. I want to talk." He glanced at Mom. "Mind if we go into the living room to speak alone?"

Elena looked at her mother for help, but she merely shrugged and turned toward the stove. Damn, she'd have to deal with Ron herself whether she liked it or not. "All right, but I have work to do. I can only give you a few minutes."

She began to follow him into the other room then stopped. "Mom, you haven't taken your nap, you must be tired. Why don't you go lie down?"

Her mother nodded. "Soon."

She didn't want her mom to feel like she had to be on guard. "I'll be all right," she said, unconvinced by her own words. The last time she'd seen Ron, she'd vowed to never speak with him again. She had grown tired of the intimidation and threats. He seemed to think he could force her to love him, to be submissive, but his bullying behavior created the opposite effect. The more aggressive he became, the more she wanted to get away from him.

She had thought about approaching him about the Vandasillo power plant. Ron had enough clout with the company to be able to make a difference. Since she hadn't had any luck with Rhoades, Ron could be her only possible advocate. But her sense that he wouldn't help her and might even be angry with her for asking, made her reticent to try. But now that he was here in person, it only made sense to do what she could.

After Ron took a seat in her father's chair, Elena sat on the sofa. She turned toward him. "I don't know why you're here, but while you're here, I could use your help."

He raised a brow. "What is it?"

"It has to do with the Vandasillo power plant," she said, hardly stopping to take a breath in case he short-circuited her or changed the subject. "I have gathered evidence that they are polluting the local groundwater and are responsible for serious medical problems in the community. I would like to share what I have with you."

Ron shook his head. "I'm not here to discuss business. I don't oversee this plant. I'll have to refer you back to Harold Rhoades."

She groaned. "I've tried to deal with Rhoades, but he denies everything I've shown him. He refuses to take any action."

"Well, that's the only advice I can offer you."

"But you work with the big boys in Los Angeles. Can't you do anything more than that?"

"Nope."

She doubted that. "So, why are you here?"

"No formalities?" Ron pursed his lips. "Okay. Since you insist on going straight to the point, I'll do the same. I want you and Gabby back. I hate this damn separation from my family. I want you in my life."

She stared at him, mouth open, but his face betrayed no emotion. How could he expect to waltz back into her life after all they'd been through, without so much as a warning, and expect her to do an immediate about-face and let him back in? After all the screamed obscenities and demeaning remarks, the nights spent in tears, the days of avoidance and hiding out, and, worst of all, the threat of violence against Gabriella. She had told herself she would never again open the door to his hurt and humiliation.

"No, Ron. We're done."

He leaned forward, a pleading look in his gray eyes. "But you don't understand. I've worked on myself as you said. I've changed. I'm not the same man you remember."

All that could be true, but Elena was unconvinced. She believed most people could change, but not Ron. He was like the alcoholic and the first drink. Once he felt he had her, he didn't seem able to control his temper. Now that she was less dependent than she had been, less of a caretaker, she didn't want to take the risk of giving him another chance. She no longer needed to play mother to his angry, demanding little boy to feel like a woman. "I'm sure you have, but I'm different, too." She made a conscious effort to soften her voice. "It's too late for us."

A creak of the front door and it sprang open. Her father limped in with Gabriella and Sal. At the sight of Ron, Dad froze.

"Ron, what a surprise. We haven't seen you in more than one harvest."

"Hello, Arturo. How's that leg?" Ron pointed to Arturo's arthritic knee.

"Better, but I still look like a carousel pony when I walk, eh, *mi nièta*?" He ruffled Gabby's hair.

Gabriella didn't answer. Instead, she stared at Ron. Sensing her fear, Sal growled for the first time in years, baring his teeth at Ron. This only added to Gabriella's confusion and she ran to hide behind Elena.

She took her daughter by the arm and drew her near. "There there, sweetie. Your dad has stopped by to see how you're doing."

Gabriella's caramel-colored skin had taken on an ashen pallor and her eyes remained fixed on Ron.

Dad waved at Gabby. "Come. Let's go into the kitchen and round up some soft drinks. A beer, Ron?"

Elena shook her head vigorously, but her father failed to notice. The last thing she needed was to encourage Ron with an excuse for staying longer.

"Love one," Ron replied.

"Come, *mi nièta*. Let's get the drinks," Dad said.

Gabby hesitated, then tiptoed out from behind Elena and started past Ron, but before she went too far, he stopped her with a hand on her arm. "Look what I bought for you." He pulled a box out of a brown paper sack and handed it to her.

She met Elena's eyes with a look of uncertainty.

"Take it, Gabby. I bought it for you." Ron shook the box at her.

Gabriella took the box and slowly peeled off the wrapping paper decorated with sprites and nymphs in a rainbow of colors. She withdrew a porcelain doll, the kind she had always wanted. The doll had long blonde hair and was dressed in white with lace and ribbons.

Gabby held the doll out. "Look, Mommy. Isn't she beautiful?"

A prickle of what she could only describe as fear flitted through Elena. Did Ron really think he could buy his daughter back? "She's gorgeous."

"Are you coming, Gabby?" Dad asked.

"In a minute, Papa. I want to play with my doll."

By the time Mom awoke from her nap, Gabriella had undressed and dressed Cecily—the name she had given her new doll—at least twice. She sat at Ron's feet and chatted happily with him. Ron and Dad had both polished off two beers and, in between paying attention to Gabby, had watched a Lakers game on ESPN.

Elena had observed the scene unfolding in front of her, trying desperately to process what she saw. They had all acted like one big happy family and she was stunned with how chummy her father was with Ron and how relaxed Gabby seemed.

Even with a healthy dose of skepticism, Elena had begun to question her own evaluation of her ex. As he playfully poked at Gabby's ribs and shared sports statistics with her father, she was amazed at how naturally he fit into the family, as though he was a missing puzzle piece that slipped right back into place.

With her shining eyes and broad smile, Gabby looked so pleased. In her denial, Elena had not realized how much the child missed her father. Gabby put the doll down and crawled onto Ron's lap, laying her head against his chest. The sight was both touching and threatening at the same time. Elena's earlier conflict reasserted itself. Had she made the right choice in leaving Ron? Was she wrong to deprive Gabriella of a full-time father? Perhaps she had overreacted and should have tried to work things out with him.

If Ron's behavior was any indicator, he seemed to have genuinely changed. But was that actually possible? Perhaps she should give him another chance. If not for her sake, at least for Gabby's. But it was premature to make any decisions.

After a surprisingly pleasant family dinner, Ron gathered up his keys. "Elena, would you mind walking me to my car?"

"Not at all," she said, and for the first time in a long time, meant it. She excused herself and strolled by his side to the Chrysler convertible.

By the car, he reached into the passenger's seat and pulled out a long, narrow box, handed it to her.

"Here's a little something for you. I didn't want to give it to you earlier in case you saw it as a bribe, but I hope you'll accept it now."

"I don't know."

"Please, Elena. No strings attached. It would mean the world to me."

The sincerity in his eyes reassured her. He kept the pressure on the box in her hand until she took and opened it. As she tore open the lid, she gasped at the diamond and gold tennis bracelet inside. "I can't accept this."

She began to hand the box back to him, but he pushed her hand away. "Of course you can. Your birthday was last month and I missed it. This is your birthday gift."

"No, I can't."

He pressed a finger to her lips. "I'm not taking it back."

"But—" Before she could protest further, he lowered himself into his car and sped off, leaving her behind staring wide-eyed at the bracelet.

She stood for a long time in the same spot, not quite knowing what to do next. She hoped he understood that even if she accepted the bracelet, it didn't mean she was taking him back. Even if he appeared more capable of being a loving husband and father than he ever had, that still remained to be seen.

***

"What are you doing here?" Elena asked, surprised to see Adam walking toward her as she locked her office door to leave work the next afternoon.

"Stopped by to see if I could talk you into a cup of coffee at El Rancho."

Elena laughed. "Have you ever tried their coffee? Dishwater is preferable. But I might join you for a cup of tea."

"Tea it is." He took her arm and led her the block to the café. Inside, the same emaciated waitress who served them before escorted them to a booth by the window. Elena slipped in across from Adam and ordered a mint tea. He took a chance and ordered the coffee.

"So," she started. "You still haven't explained the unexpected visit."

The waitress placed steaming cups in front of them. Elena opened the packet of tea and placed it in the hot water.

Adam took a sip from his cup and made a face. "*This* is a big notch below dishwater. Closer to sewage, if I can say that in public."

"Told you so." Elena smiled at him. He looked so adorable in his turquoise polo shirt, his wavy hair long enough to curl around the collar. She wished she didn't find him so damn attractive. "Now answer my question."

Adam placed his cup on the table. All around them the buzz of activity and people talking filled the air. Kids chased one another past their table, nearly knocking into it.

"I've been doing a lot of thinking since I last saw you. I'm in a funny position. While I've been hired to represent the power company, I'm not antagonistic to your concerns."

"I'm glad."

"But I believe the company has a stronger case with documented analysis to back it up."

She watched him over the cup, watched the lines deepen between his brows, not at all comfortable with the direction this was taking.

"Studies that may be biased for all we know."

"But which are a far cry from superstition or hysteria."

Elena lowered the cup, then nodded to the woman who ran the dry goods store. "So what exactly are you trying to say?"

"I'm worried about you, Elena. You seem to be on a private campaign that is leading straight into the jaws of hell. I think your quest to finger the power company has become an obsession, and it's neither healthy or helpful."

Anger choked her. *I thought he was going to be more sympathetic. Instead, he thinks I'm crazy.* "Do you think I'm nuts?"

He lifted a hand. "No, of course not. I'm saying that in your zeal to help others, you've talked yourself into believing something that isn't real. That's all." He rubbed his brow between thumb and forefinger. "I met with Rhoades and told him what happened with your car. He thinks one or more of the workers might be behind it. They depend on their jobs for a living. They have spouses and kids to feed. If they feel threatened, who can tell what they might do. I don't want anything bad happening to you." A shake of his head emphasized his words.

Her anger hardened and she swallowed it down. "So Rhoades put you up to this. What are you, his puppet? Aren't you able to think for yourself, or is he buying you with a paycheck?"

Adam's face flushed a deep red. "Look, I work for Rhoades, whether that meets with your approval or not, but I still have my principles. If you can prove the plant's to blame for the community's problems, I'd certainly take this up with the company. But so far the only evidence I've seen isn't too persuasive."

He reached across the table and enclosed Elena's hand in his. She tried to pull away, but he held on. "I'm genuinely concerned about your well-being. I don't think your actions are doing you any good or making you any friends."

He held her eyes and a fluttering feeling filled her. She couldn't allow her attraction for him to influence her.

When she was able to pull her hand back, she said, "If you're an example of a friend, I don't need others."

The hurt in his eyes stopped her for a moment.

"You're too obvious, Adam. All you're concerned about is your job. Nothing you can say will dissuade me from pursuing the power plant until I'm convinced they aren't at fault for what's going on in the community. In the meantime, I'm fully prepared to face any consequences my actions stir up." Riled up by what she took as his betrayal, she glared at him.

He gestured for the waitress. "You are too damn stubborn, Elena. I only hope you don't create a storm you can't stop."

The waitress came by their table and gave Adam the check. He rummaged in his wallet and handed her a five-dollar bill.

"Keep the change."

Elena was about to slide out of the booth when she spotted Ron weaving his way to their table. She froze and could hear the pounding of her pulse in her head. Her eyes met Adam's.

"What's wrong?" His gaze followed hers to Ron as he approached.

She placed a hand on the table to steady herself. "What are you doing here?"

Ron's eyes flickered over her face then fixed on Adam. As he spoke his gaze never left Adam's face.

"Same thing you are. Having lunch. But that doesn't look like the only thing you're doing."

She had to intervene to dispel the tension. "Ron, this is Adam Slater. He's a lawyer for the local power company. We're working on a problem together." She could only hope this explanation would extinguish the fire in Ron's eyes.

"A lawyer, huh? So you're one of *those* assholes." Ron spoke so loudly that conversation ceased at the tables around them and everyone stared.

Elena's gut fluttered with fear. She wrapped her arms around herself. "This meeting is purely professional. Please don't make this a personal issue."

Ron's eyes took on a demonic gleam. "Why should I believe you, you slut. You've always lied to me. You've been sleazing around behind my back for years."

Flabbergasted by the unexpected violence of his words, she recoiled, then felt ashamed at how quickly she slipped into her old behavior around him.

Adam sprang to his feet and placed himself between Ron and her. "How dare you speak to Elena that way."

Ron's eyes flared with fury, a fury she well remembered. He shoved Adam, but Adam stood his ground.

"Get out of my way. I'm talking to my wife."

Adam poked a finger into Ron's ribs. "Ex-wife, from what I've heard. But no matter, you have no right to treat anyone that way."

Elena had somehow managed to stumble to her feet and stood by Adam's side. "Let's take this outside."

Ron glared at her. "Why? Are you afraid to face me here?"

Elena swallowed down her rising fear, "No. Not at all." She glanced around at the up-turned faces and shocked expressions. Clearly, Ron was determined to humiliate her. "If you want to make this a public spectacle, so be it." She folded her arms over her chest. She had enough of his intimidation. She wouldn't take it anymore. For too long, she had tried to keep the peace. Be understanding. Mature. Ron had met his Waterloo in her resolve to no longer endure his abuse. She wouldn't let him defeat her again.

With the secure knowledge that Adam was by her side, she held Ron's eyes. "I won't tolerate your accusations and name-calling anymore. Whatever you say, you haven't changed at all. You're acting exactly like you always have." She defiantly raised her chin. "Now I want you to pack your bags and go back to Los Angeles. Leave Gabby and me alone. We're doing fine without the upset and anger in our lives."

Ron's face set in the mask-like threatening grimace that always scared the hell out of her. "You're unfit to be a mother. Running around with every man in sight. You tramp. I'll go all right, to find myself a lawyer and get my daughter away from you."

"The hell you will."

Ron grabbed her shoulder and pinched it. When she yelped, Adam grasped Ron's arm and thrust it away from her.

"Don't be a fool. Elena already has the best representation available. If you think you can beat us, I'd love to see it."

Ron's face a dark crimson. He could only gape at Adam.

"Why you..." Ron stuttered. The look he gave Elena was deadly.

"We'll see about that." He began to back off then halted. "If you think you've heard the last of me, you're wrong."

Elena stared him down. She stuck her hand in her pocket and immediately remembered the bracelet at home. "You've already heard the last of me except for the bracelet. I'll mail it to your post office box first thing tomorrow."

Ron's face was a caricature of rage and, for the first time, she could see how ridiculous and helpless he really looked. A small child throwing a temper tantrum because he couldn't get what he wanted. She almost expected him to stamp his feet. Instead, he stormed out the door, and let it slam shut behind him.

After a few moments, Elena slid back into the booth and waited until the patrons gradually turned back to their conversations. The noise level cloaked her, made her feel safe. She met Adam's eyes. "Do you think he meant what he said?"

"I doubt it. He's probably bluffing. But don't worry, there's nothing he can do and he knows it. You're through with him, which is good because you have bigger monsters to tame."

She blotted the moisture beading her brow. Did Adam mean the power plant or her mother's illness? Or was it her affection for him?

At that moment it all blended into a huge knot of anxiety.

Chapter 18

Elena set the receiver into its cradle and looked up to see Herman Molar in the office doorway. He shifted from one foot to the other as though uncertain whether to stay or go. Before he could leave, she rose to her feet and greeted him. "Come in. It's been a long time."

He hesitated a moment longer, then entered the office.

"Have a seat." She gestured at a chair on the other side of the desk. "What brings you in today?"

"I..." Herman bit at a hangnail. "I don't mean ta disturb yuse, but I stopped by da plant, saw my old boss, asked for severance pay."

Curiosity aroused, Elena leaned forward. "What did he tell you?"

"Thad they'd be glad ta give me the dough but they'd only do it if I signed a statement."

"What kind of statement?"

Herman nibbled at the nail. "Da kinda statement what says I won't say nothin' about da plant ever to anyone."

Elena nodded to encourage him.

"I coulda signed it. Walked away with da dough, but somethin' held me back. I don't know whad it was. I jus' couldn't sign it."

Elena sat perfectly still, not wanting to pressure him or scare him off. "Do you have something to tell me?"

"It was like when my fuckin' stepfather did tha' thing to my sister and I was too scared to say somethin'. I get so mad thinkin' about it. I shoulda done somethin'."

"Where's your sister now?"

"She overdosed. Offed herself. I shoulda done somethin', but I didn't do nothin' to help her." Herman lowered his head to his hands.

Elena moved around the desk and laid a hand on his shoulder. "You were young. You didn't know what to do."

Herman jerked his head up and stared at her. "I can't save her, but I can do somethin' now." He turned to stare out the window a long moment, then took a deep breath. "There's a piece of equipment west of the plant. I heard one of the guys call it an oil-water separator, but hell if I know what it does."

She squeezed his shoulder. "And?"

"Behind it is a leach field for the stuff that flows through it. All I knows is what I saw. There's been some activity out there, some suits even walkin' around. And I overheard one of the night crew say 'don't let the state catch ya doin' that.'"

"Doing what?"

"Look, I ain't no engineer. I'm jus' a thug. Get it? I can jus' tell yuse what I saw."

Elena followed his gaze to the fields beyond the window. "You think there might be a problem with this piece of equipment?"

Herman didn't answer but continued to stare past her.

"And they're covering it up?" Elena prompted.

"Yeah. Tha's what I think." He clenched his fist. "It stinks," he hissed and bent over, resting elbows on knees, lowering his head. "I wish I coulda jus' taken that dough and ran."

Elena didn't know whether to feel triumphant or fearful. She patted him on the back. "You're a good man, Herman Molar. I always knew you were." She continued to pat him until he looked up and gave her a wan smile.

"Shit. I'm in this way deep."

"We're in this together and don't you ever forget that."

"Whaddya yuse plan to do?"

Elena leaned back against the desk, supporting herself with hands at both sides. "Go to Sacramento to report what I learned. What you told me only confirms the tests I've already done. Hopefully, this gives me enough ammunition to convince them to send an inspector of their own."

Herman slowly lifted his head. "I sure as hell hope they do. It's time to fry the bastards." He scrunched up his face as though surprised by the strength of his own response. "Don't ya worry. I'll back yuse all the way."

Elena stood up. "I knew from the first time I met you behind the plant I could rely on you, Herman. And, don't you worry either. Whatever happens, I'm on your side, too."

Herman's eyes held sad wisdom. "Yuse remind me of my sister, Elena. I couldn't let her down another time."

"I know she'd think you were brave for what you're doing today and so do I."

"I only wish she was here to see it."

***

"Nice of you to offer, but you really don't have to go. It's a long trip to Sacramento. I can handle the EPA all by my lonesome." Elena's voice was soft but insistent.

Adam felt a ping of annoyance. He didn't want to miss out on this meeting for the world. Besides, he needed to be there. "Wrong. I have to go. I'm representing the power plant. Someone needs to be there from their camp. That's my job."

"All right, if you insist." Elena sighed. "Have it your way, but I have to go in the morning. It was a challenge to arrange this meeting so I can't reschedule."

"I'll work at rescheduling my appointments and pick you up at seven."

Silence met his words.

"And Elena..."

"Yes?"

He had to convince her of his sincerity. "Remember that whatever happens, I'm not the enemy."

"I'll try to keep that in mind."

***

Elena glanced around the EPA guy's office and noted the lack of color or creativity. It looked exactly like she imagined a bureaucrat's office would. Navajo white walls with a couple of framed diplomas, a picture of the guy shaking the governor's hand and, on the far wall, a commendation from the President of the United States for his work at the EPA. On his desk, an open file and a glass paperweight. Beyond, a metal file cabinet: nothing distinctive or original. Everything temporary, plain, added without any serious consideration, like the guy himself in his gray suit and blue tie.

As a representative of the Environmental Protection Agency, John Ratan's voice droned on about toxic levels and conflicting results, sounding inconclusive, unconvinced. "Obviously your report contradicts the power company's, but the power plant had an independent firm conduct their studies, Ms. Marquez. While you certainly have an agenda, I spoke with Harold Rhoades myself this morning and he's willing to further investigate your allegations without involving us."

Elena's hopes, so buoyant before, had slowly sunk under the weight of Ratan's words. "But I have more than the studies to back up my claims. Did you read Mr. Molar's report?"

Ratan knitted his brows. "Of course, but I have to weigh in the fact that he's a disgruntled ex-employee, recently fired. That doesn't exactly make him an unbiased witness."

After all this, to be shoved aside like so much river silt would be unbearable. She seemed to be losing ground by the minute. Tears of frustration burned at the back of her throat.

This meeting was her last, best chance to convince the state to take action and it was turning into an abysmal failure. "But he's willing to testify in a court of law if necessary."

"That doesn't alter the facts, Ms. Marquez. I'm not sure the EPA should be investing its limited resources into this wild goose chase." Ratan took a sip from a Styrofoam cup. "What do you think, Mr. Slater? You represent the company. Do you believe it's necessary to involve the EPA here? Spend the taxpayers' dollars on this?"

Adam refused to meet her eyes, which made her all the more uncomfortable. She squirmed in the padded seat. He could make or break Ratan's decision.

Adam cleared his throat. "As an attorney for the power company, I would caution you that you will be wasting your time. The company is more than willing to police itself and it would be redundant to do more than we're already doing."

Ratan bobbed his head in concert with Adam's words and Elena's broken heart now splintered. With a few words, he had not only spoiled the opportunity for a fair and impartial investigation of the power plant, but he had ended any hope of a relationship between them.

How could she ever trust him again if he was so willing to betray her now? Everything inside her cried out to him, pleaded with him, begged him not to destroy the fragile feelings developing between them, but she had nowhere to turn. She looked away from him, not wanting to face the glow of triumph on his face. It would be the final blow.

With the roaring in her ears, she could barely hear Adam's next words.

"But as a representative of humanity, I think you owe it to everyone to do a government-run study. This is too serious a matter to be given short shrift. If, as I believe, Valley View Gas and Electric is innocent of the charges asserted by Ms. Marquez, they should be thrilled to have the EPA's confirmation they're not polluting the water and put to rest the rumors running through the community. If I'm wrong and they're at fault, the community deserves to know the truth so the problem can be rectified before anyone else's health is compromised."

She could hardly believe her ears and had to suppress the urge to ask him to repeat himself. Before she could react, Ratan sat forward, a surprised expression on his flat face.

"That's a strong endorsement for the government's intervention, coming from you." He sat back and grinned. "I have to tell you that makes my job easier. If you're both in agreement that we should send inspectors, it's a done deal." He looked directly at Elena. "You're a pretty persuasive person, Ms. Marquez. Your persistence in this matter has paid off. We'll send a team to Vandasillo next week."

***

Elena left the meeting first, a lilt in her step and a smile creasing her lips. Victory. She could dance a jig. At last, she had moved the mountain of doubt and resistance that had plagued her progress. She had what she wanted. And she couldn't have done it without Adam.

A block down the street, she pulled him into an alcove beneath an awning and threw her arms around his neck. "Thank you, thank you, thank you," she whispered into his ear, sensing a shiver of desire run through him.

He drew her closer and kissed her neck, sending a similar shiver through her. "I only did what I believed was right."

"You're a man of principle, Adam Slater, and I admire you for that."

"And you're a woman of principles, Elena Marquez, and I love you for that."

Her breath caught in her throat and, for a moment, she couldn't speak. Then she pulled back and looked into his eyes to see if he was teasing. The intensity of his gaze caused her to sway. As she grabbed his shirt to right herself, he lowered his lips onto hers and her mouth opened and yielded to his touch. His lips were warm, soft and insistent. The longer she kissed the more she wanted him.

The echo of footsteps on pavement and the rustle of movement outside their window reminded her they were on a busy downtown street. She pulled back enough to look into his eyes. "Since it's late and I already told my folks I may have to spend the night, would you like to get a room?"

He ran fingers through her hair and brought her face to his, then lowered his lips to the nape of her neck. She could feel the warmth of him, and smell the scent of him. Her breath caught in her throat. Now she knew what they meant when they said someone could take your breath away. He certainly took hers.

"I'd love it," he said, voice husky with desire.

"I did an Internet search before we left. There's a hotel a couple of blocks from here."

He chuckled. "Always the consummate girl scout, you're prepared." Gently, he ran his lips against her cheek and sent a stream of sensation trailing his movement. "That's another thing I love about you."

"I love hearing you say those things." She took his hand. "Follow me."

"Anywhere."

***

The hotel was a modern-looking building with smoked glass windows and massive bronze doors. Elena would normally have spent time exploring the multi-level lobby displaying large abstract canvases and a Thomas Moore-type sculpture in the center, but she could hardly wait to register and have Adam all to herself.

As soon as the bellhop closed the door to the room behind him, she rushed into Adam's open arms. The kiss they shared was deep with longing. An eternity had passed since his visit when she felt anything even close to the intensity of sensation his kiss ignited, along with the emotions he aroused. She luxuriated in the embrace.

After that kiss came another then another until he drew back and cocked his head to the side in an endearing gesture. His fingertips gently touched her face and brushed away an errant strand of hair. "You're so lovely. I've wanted this for a long, long time. As long as I've known you."

"Come here." She led him over to the king-sized bed, where she sat on the edge and pulled him to sit beside her.

Once again, he ran fingers over her face, her hair, then down her neck. "I want you, Elena. More than I ever imagined I could want anyone." With those words he lowered his lips to hers and kissed her with as much ardor as she'd ever known, dizzying her, making her hunger for more. In turn, she leaned back and drew him on top of her, all the while kissing his head, combing fingers through thick curly hair.

His breathing had deepened, and his skin had heated to her touch. As he continued to kiss his way down her chest, to lift her blouse and move aside her bra, to lick her nipple and stroke her, she writhed and groaned beneath him. Her desire for him, intense before, had become almost unbearable. Quickly, she removed what remained of her clothing, as did he. Naked, she reached over and drew him onto her, into her.

She'd wanted them to go slow, to savor the moment, but when he started to move inside her, they lost control. Mouths, hands, kissing, licking, nipping, touching became a frenzy of sensations that overtook her. Time was suspended and nothing and no one else mattered or existed. A radiant heat filled her core, and like an exploding star, she rained her sparks over him as he held her tight, his warm breath caressing her ear as his body confirmed the words he'd whispered over and over.

Chapter 19

"And have you heard about Alfredo's ulcer?" Maria Rodriquez asked.

Elena shook her head. Even Maria's many concerns and complaints didn't dampen Elena's high spirits. She was in love. Pure shout from the rooftops, skip down the street, unadulterated love. Love with a capital L. She wanted to embrace Maria, take her hands and pull her to her feet and dance her around the room while singing the Beatles tune "All You Need is Love" at the top of her lungs. *Lighten up*, she almost said to Maria, but knew better and held her tongue. She didn't want to bring anyone down. Not today.

"It is terrible for Rolanda," Maria whined.

"I imagine, but ulcers aren't the end of the world."

The phone rang, giving her a chance to end this disturbing discussion. Elena lifted the receiver. "Yes?"

"Do you have a moment to talk?" Adam asked.

Elena's face flushed hot with excitement. "Of course. Hold on one moment." She placed a palm over the receiver. "Would you mind if I take this long-distance call?"

Maria patted a wad of tissue at her damp forehead. "All right, but I will be back on Thursday when we come to town for feed. I have more to tell." Maria rose.

"Do that." Elena waited for Maria to close the office door, before uncovering the phone, anxious to hear what had happened to Adam in Los Angeles. "How are you?"

"Not too good."

He worried her. She nibbled her lip while waiting to hear more.

"I've been fired. I'm officially unemployed."

The flush turned to fire and, all at once, the ground wobbled beneath her feet. "They can't do that. It's unfair."

"Unfair or not, they did it."

Guilt and worry stabbed at her, making her stomach churn. "But—but, what happened?"

"Rhoades got to Douglass Lubbock before I did. He threatened to find another firm to represent him if they didn't replace me. Douglass agreed to send my ex-fiancée's latest victim in my place. She found herself another aspiring attorney to marry and has arranged to have him sent to Siberia."

"Is that really how you see Vandasillo?"

"Sorry. I did at first. Not any longer. But that's how the firm views you." He paused and took a deep breath. "Anyway, Douglass said that after what happened in Vandasillo they no longer need my services. Boom. He fired me."

Elena's throat had tightened with guilt so that she could hardly respond. This was all her fault. But what could she have done differently? She had a community to protect. "Is there any recourse?"

"A good moving truck. I can probably appeal the decision, but I don't know what that would mean for my career. It wouldn't exactly look good on my CV."

Elena choked on the thought. Her earlier elation had turned to remorse. "Oh, Adam. I'm so sorry. Is there anything I can do to help?"

He cleared his throat. "Try to understand that I won't be able to return to Vandasillo for a while. I need to stick around here and dust myself off, look for another position. It will take some time, but I'll keep in touch."

Her head spun with worry for him. "What if I come to you, help you out? I write a mean letter. I can type, cook, you name it."

"No. I need to do this myself."

She cringed at the coldness in his voice. He blamed her as much as she blamed herself. And as long as he held her responsible, he'd want nothing to do with her. A tear ran down her cheek, but she brushed it aside. "I feel horrible. I wish this hadn't happened."

"Me too, but it did. Look, I have to go. There's a guy here to help me move my files."

She stifled a sob. "Okay. Will you call?"

"Sure. I'll ring you in a day or two." The line clicked close with the finality of failure.

Elena sat upright by the desk, grasping the receiver to her chest. All her hopes, all her dreams, all her plans ground to rubble with one short call. And Adam? What about his dreams? His future? His career? A cascade of tears followed the thought.

By the time she looked up, dusk was leaving and night was taking its place. How long had she been sitting at her desk? How would she manage to lock up and stumble to her car? She forced herself to stand and her legs to move. Thank heavens for routine. Practice. With heavy legs and a staggering gait, she made her way out of the building.

On her way home, blind to the road or the cars around her, she made up her mind. It wouldn't be fair to hurt Adam anymore. He was absolutely right staying away from her. She was the source of his problem. No matter the cost, she would never again cause him any pain.

***

"Anyone home?" Adam stuck his head through the open door of the Marquez house. He looked around, found the kitchen empty. No one answered his call. "Hello," he yelled louder.

Frieda's feeble, "Come in," drifted out from the living room. She rested on the sofa, a pillow beneath her head, a blanket pulled up to her chin. Although pale, her eyes were as lively as ever.

"Hello, Adam," she said. "Elena isn't home."

His smile covered disappointment. "Too bad I missed her, but I also came to see you. How're you doing?"

She gestured toward Arturo's chair. "Please sit."

She tried to raise herself on an elbow, but he motioned that she continued resting. "Don't exert yourself."

"What kind of host would I be if I didn't offer you a drink?"

His smile was now inward. To think she'd be this concerned with social graces in her condition. He wagged his finger. "How could you ever be less than gracious? Besides, I know where you keep the cups and the endless pot of coffee. If I want one, I can help myself."

"But—"

"You said I was a part of this family. You have to let me act it."

Frieda's pasty face took on a hint of color. "You win this time, but next time you have to let me serve you." Her shoulders slumped and she let her head fall back against the armrest.

"That's only a deal if you're feeling better. Have you heard anything from Fresno? What's the diagnosis?"

A smile curled the corners of Frieda's lips. "They believe I'm severely anemic and don't have leukemia."

In his enthusiasm, Adam reached out, grabbed her soft hand. "That's great." He held her hand until she pulled hers back.

"It would be if they wouldn't insist on so much bed rest and those giant-sized iron pills three times a day." A pill bottle sat on its side near her head. "They're so big the horses would have trouble swallowing them."

Relief washed over him. He clapped his hands in glee. "All right."

"Now you all have to start treating me like a normal person again. I'm not made of clay. I won't break."

She couldn't know how fragile she looked. "How about the exhaustion?"

"The doctor says I'll feel stronger in a couple of weeks. In the meantime, he wants me tied to this sofa during the day." A pat on the pillow followed her words. "But I'm so glad you're here." She stretched out a hand toward him. "I'm worried about Elena."

A vise gripped his chest, making it hard to breathe. It had been a couple of weeks since he last saw her. "Is anything wrong? What's going on?"

"She was so upset when she heard about your being fired. She felt so responsible. Elena's too good. She cares too much about others, especially you." Frieda's eyes met his in a moment of understanding deeper than words.

He could have laughed and cried simultaneously. Isn't this what he had wanted more than air to breathe, water to drink? "I love her, Frieda, and I'd do anything for her."

"I know you do." Her smile felt like a blessing he so needed. "Because you do, I'm going to do something I've never done before." She sighed. "Elena asked me not to tell anyone where she'd gone, but I'm going to break that promise." She reached over and took a sip of water.

He held his breath.

"She left for the Sierras, said she needed to be alone. Left Gabby with us."

"Do you need any help?"

Frieda flapped her hand. "This is too important. Now listen." She shot him an exasperated look. "I know where Elena is staying. There are cabins just outside of King's Canyon. I wrote the information down." She reached behind her then hesitated. "I wouldn't tell anyone else, but I know she needs to talk with you."

In the late afternoon light streaming in through the voile curtains on the west window, Frieda's face lit up in bas-relief. A wonderful face. A face he loved. She had come to represent the mother he wished he had. Loving, attentive, consistent and supportive. The Marquez family had come to be the family he always wanted. He no longer envied Elena her family because they had become his family, too.

He bent over Frieda and wrapped her in his arms. "Thank you," he whispered into her fresh-scented hair. "You'll never have to regret doing this."

She nodded her head against him. "I know that, too." She gave him a gentle push against his arm. "Now go to Elena and bring her home to us."

***

Adam reached the King's Canyon Cabins in record time: three hours later. A large cabin acted as the check-in/reception area. He went over to the front desk to inquire about Elena's room number. The clerk was busy with a Southern California couple who were demanding a different cabin because theirs was not up to their SoCal standards. Adam stood to the side, watching this show of arrogance with amusement. Once they settled on a more appropriately appointed room and paid the difference, he stepped up to the counter.

"I'm trying to reach a Ms. Elena Marquez. She should have checked in earlier today."

"Are you family?" the clerk asked.

"Yes, I'm her brother," Adam lied, to ensure he could reach her. "I'm here as planned to pick her up for dinner."

The clerk studied him, then glanced down at his reservation book. "Let's see. She's in Baby Bear." He turned to look at the key rack behind him. "The keys are still here. She hasn't checked in yet."

That surprised him because Frieda had said she left Vandasillo in the morning. "Oh, okay. Is it all right if I wait for her in the lobby?" He pointed toward a small cluster of chairs around a stone fireplace.

The clerk shrugged. "Suit yourself."

Adam took a seat in an overstuffed faux leather chair and put his feet up on an ottoman. He was a bit concerned, but knowing Elena it wouldn't be surprising if she stopped to see a client or help someone out before leaving town. He leaned his head back against the cushion and closed his eyes to rest them.

When he opened them again and glanced at his watch it was ninety minutes later. He stretched, unnerved that he had fallen asleep and missed Elena when she arrived. He had been hoping to catch her before she had a chance to take off into the woods.

He approached the desk again. The same clerk sat reading the local rag. Adam cleared his throat. "Has the woman in Baby Bear already checked in?"

The clerk shook his bald head. "Not since I've been here."

An alarm went off in Adam's head. It was almost six and no sign of Elena. Now he was worried. "You're sure of that?"

"Of course I'm sure. I've been here all afternoon."

Adam went back to his newfound favorite chair and pulled out his phone.

He dialed her number, but the phone went to voicemail. He left her a message. Still worried, he knew he had to do more. Although he didn't want to alarm Frieda, he had to find out if Elena had changed her mind and returned home. He dialed the Marquez house and Gabby answered.

"Hi Gabby. Is your Mama around?"

"Uh-uh," Gabby said hesitantly. "She's gone."

"Okay, I'll call back another time." Adam hung up, relieved he hadn't had to worry Frieda, but more frantic than ever about Elena. What if she had a car accident? Lost her way? Or worse?

Since she was only four hours later than expected, the police would probably scoff at his concern, but he'd couldn't afford to wait much longer to contact them. He had to file a report.

As it was, he paced the lobby and called everyone he could, hoping to locate her, but had no luck. Finally, at eight p.m., he contacted the police, who took a statement, but said they wouldn't file it as a missing person until she had been gone for at least forty-eight hours. The cop at the other end of the line told him to call back at that time.

Too agitated to rest, he paced the floor to calm his nerves before he could concoct other ideas for locating her. He called her phone yet again, but still no answer. Finally, after the clerk asked him to stop pacing and gave him permission to spend a few more hours on the overstuffed chair, he found a pad and a pen and began furiously scribbling notes. He recognized this might be futile, but it was the only thing he could do to channel his anxiety.

Between entries marked with bullet points, he would look up at his watch, then over toward the entrance door. The agonizing wait made every second drag on. At ten o'clock he asked the night clerk if he could wait for Elena a while longer. Then he called her for the tenth time before going outside for a breather.

The crisp night air felt refreshing but did nothing to quiet the panic growing inside of him. What if something terrible had happened to her? Would he ever forgive himself for not being available to her?

He wracked his brain for answers, but the only thoughts that appeared led him deeper and deeper into despair.

Chapter 20

Morning light crept through cracks between lobby shutters. Adam had hardly slept. He had caught a few winks on the faux leather lounge chair with his lower legs and feet elevated on the ottoman, but every movement, every sound, every rustle of leaves outside jolted him into immediate awareness. Instantly awake, he searched his surrounding, checking in with the clerk and calling Elena's number one more time.

Not able to reach her, he was beyond distraught. He was in full panic mode.

After splashing his face and gurgling water, he headed back to town, not knowing what he would do when he arrived, or who he might pursue for information. He had no sooner turned down Main Street than he spotted Herman Molar leaving the coffee shop. While he had never met the man, Elena had shared his story with Adam and pointed him out one day when they walked past the Squeaky Clean Car Wash where Molar was working at the time. Adam knew that Molar had been helpful to Elena in the past.

He pulled the car to the curb in front of Molar, jumped out and flagged him down. "Hi, Herman. I'm a friend of Elena Marquez and I could use your help."

Molar looked surprised. "I don't know what yuse talking about. I haven't seen Elena for days. I'm not sure how I can help yuse."

He looked as if he would move on, but Adam stepped in front of him, blocking his path. "I'm afraid Elena has been missing since yesterday. Have you seen or heard from her?"

"Oh, jeez." Molar placed his hand over his mouth. "What yuse mean, missin'?"

"I can't find her anywhere. She was supposed to have taken a break in the Sierras, but she never arrived at the cabin she booked. She's not at her family home, and I can't reach her by phone."

"Whoa," Molar said, his eyes filling with concern. "That's not good. Whaddyu think happened to her?"

"I wish I knew. I'm sick with worry, but I can't figure it out. I was hoping you might know something, but I see you don't." He handed Molar a card. "Call me if you hear anything, all right?"

Moler stared at the card. "Sure...sure." He nibbled his upper lip. "Tell yuse what...Adam. I still knows some of the guys at the plant. I'll ask them if they knows anythin'."

"I'd appreciate that. Call me either way. I want to hear what they say."

"Yeah. Sure. Yuse'll be the first to knows."

For the first time in almost twenty-four hours Adam felt a prickle of hope. Perhaps someone at the plant will know what happened to Elena. Inside he voiced a silent prayer for assistance.

He went back to his room to regroup, take a quick shower and change his day-old, slept-in clothes. After downing a cup of coffee, he considered his options. He decided his best course of action was to retrace the steps as there wasn't any evidence. He called the plant and made an appointment to meet with Harold Rhoades.

An hour later, he took a seat across the desk from Rhoades.

Rhoades waited a moment, then said, "So what brings you here today?"

Adam sat forward. "Elena Marquez is missing, and I don't know where to look for her."

Rhoades shrugged. "What does that have to do with me?"

Intrigued with Rhoades's lack of response, Adam studied him. "That doesn't seem to concern you at all."

"It's not that I'm not concerned, it's that I'm not surprised. With her campaign to expose the plant for wrongdoing, she's upset many of our workers. They're the ones concerned that if the plant has problems, they'll lose their jobs."

"So are you suggesting that workers at the plant might have kidnapped Elena to stop her from interfering in your business?"

Rhoades shook his head. "Not necessarily, but that certainly is a possibility. I personally have no idea what happened to her."

"Is there any way you can find out before I file a police report? Unless the police have something concrete to work with they will be snooping around here and might be more of a distraction than Elena ever was."

Rhoades's eyes narrowed. There was a tightness around his mouth as he said, "I'll ask around, see if anyone knows anything."

"I hope you will, because this can become a real hassle for you."

Rhoades rose abruptly. "I have another meeting. I'll let you know if I learn anything."

Adam stood. "Okay, I'll wait to hear from you." Although he suspected he would never hear from Rhoades voluntarily.

A call from Herman woke Adam from a restless nap on the sofa. It was the first time he'd been able to steal a few winks since the Sierras. He was groggy when he answered the phone. Herman's voice sounded a million miles away.

"Hey, boss, I got some news for yous."

"What—what's going on?"

"I talked to the guys over a beer a few minutes ago at the pub and they tell me one of the security guards discovered your girlfriend at the oil-water separator on Friday morning. Sez she was taking a water sample nearby. Since they was told to hold onto her if she came sneaking around, they called the head of security and he sez he was on the way to pick her up."

That news immediately caused Adam's mind to clear. "Do they know what happened to her after that?"

"Nope. According to them, the guard left as soon as the boss arrived."

"So," Adam mused, "she must still be in their custody."

"Sure sounds like it." Herman paused. "I has an idea. I still has a spare key to the security offices no one knows about. If yuse would like, we can check the area out."

"Yes, I'd like that. How soon can we meet?"

Chapter 21

An hour later, Adam watched as a white Dodge Dart with a green hood pulled up alongside his parked Jeep. He got in alongside Herman, who drove to the entrance of the power company. Herman had borrowed credentials from one of the other off-duty guards. He wore a cap over his close-cut hair. With sunglasses, his disguise was pretty convincing. After a few tense moments while the gate guard studied the tag, they were allowed onto the property.

They drove up to the main building, which housed administration and security. After parking, Herman let him into the bottom floor. They walked down a long hallway. Since it was after dark, the building was empty, and they didn't need to explain their presence to anyone. At the rear of the building, they entered an office marked Chief of Security.

Herman produced a key to the office. "Lucky for yuse I kept my keys."

"I'd be luckier if I knew where Elena was and I wasn't sneaking into offices to find her."

"Yeah, I guess yuse right about that."

When Herman flicked on a light, Adam could see the cluttered room with the enormous wooden desk strewn with various files. On the wall behind the desk was a row of computer monitors. "Wow, where do we start?"

"And what are we lookin' for?"

Adam paused to collect his thoughts. "I'd say anything that would prove Elena's been here."

Herman went over to the file cabinet and began rifling through it. Although uncomfortable with the idea of going through another man's documents, Adam proceeded to look through the files on the desk and then opened one drawer after another. In the bottom drawer he spotted something familiar and pulled it out. It was a black appointment book identical to the one Elena used. He flipped open the cover and saw the writing. It was Elena's. "Look at this."

Herman joined him by the desk. "What is it, boss?"

"It's Elena's. She's been here and, since she carries that book with her everywhere, it must have been recently."

"Oh man," Herman said. "So my friend was right. She was picked up by security. Now to figure where they took her."

Adam's heart raced with the thought she could be nearby. "Is there anywhere around here where she could be confined?"

Herman nodded. "Alls I can think of is the storeroom?"

"Show it to me."

Herman led him down another hall to a security door.

"Open it."

"I wish I could, boss, but I don't has the key. Only the head of security does. This area is off limits for the rest of us."

Adam stared at the metal door. There was no way to tear it down, but if he could get inside, Elena might be only feet from where he stood. "There has to be a way."

Herman shrugged. "Not that I knows of."

He had run into an impediment that seemed as massive and impenetrable, but he held to his conviction: where there's a will, there's a way. And he was going to find that way if it was the last thing he ever accomplished.

***

The first light of day lit up Harold Rhoades's office. Adam sat up straight in the wing-back chair by Rhoades's desk and rubbed his eyes. He'd chosen to spend the night at the power plant and not risk being refused entry in the morning. Herman had let him into Rhoades's office before leaving to catch a few winks in anticipation of another day at work.

Adam went into the restroom to splash water on his face and rinse out his mouth. He hadn't expected to spend the night at the plant or he would have brought along some supplies.

Back in the office, he made himself as small as he could in the chair and waited for Rhoades. After a time he began to hear voices and activity outside the room, then Rhoades opened the door. He said something to someone outside the room and, much to Adam's relief, shut the door. As soon as he started into the room, Adam stood.

Rhoades gasped. "What the hell are you doing here?"

"Sorry for the unannounced visit, but I need to speak with you."

Rhoades turned back toward the door. "Not now. You're on your way out. "

Adam made a lunge at Rhoades and caught him by his collar. "Not quite yet. I have some business with you."

Rhoades tried to squirm away, but Adam held on tightly. "I want to know where you've hidden Elena."

Rhoades pivoted to face him. "What? Are you crazy? I have nothing to do with her disappearance."

"Yeah," Adam said. "Then how do you explain this?" And he reached over to pluck Elena's appointment book off Rhoades's desk.

Rhoades wrinkled his brow. "What is it?"

"Her appointment book. Found it in the security office last night."

"What were you doing in security last night?"

"Long story. What are you doing with Elena's book? She would never willingly part with it since it has all her clients' information. It had to have been forcibly taken from her."

"Okay." Rhoades sighed, and, released from Adam's grip, went to his chair and took a seat. "She was here the other night."

"Under what circumstances? What was she doing here?"

"We found her snooping around the oil/water separator and we brought her in for questioning, but since we couldn't find any reason to hold onto her, we released her."

That revelation immediately caused Adam's blood pressure to rise. "What do you mean you released her? Did she drive off on her own? She hasn't been seen since. Who did you release her to?"

"Someone sent over from headquarters in Los Angeles. We wanted to cover our bases so we contacted the CEO's office. A friend of Elena's offered to pick her up and take her home."

"And what's the name of that representative?"

Harold shook his head. "I don't remember. I'll have to call security."

Adam took his seat by the desk. "You do that. I'm waiting."

Rhoades lifted the receiver and dialed a number. He asked whoever picked up the call the name in question. After a couple of minutes, he jotted something down on his telephone pad and lowered the receiver. "Ronald Samson."

Of course: it had to be Ron.

"He was supposed to take her home. I was assured he would take care of her, take her home." Lines appeared on Harold's face, lines Adam hadn't noticed before.

"Can you find me this Ronald Samson's information? I'll need to follow up on this, or the police will."

"I—I'll get it for you," Rhoades sputtered nervously. "I never meant anything to happen to her. It was never my intention."

Adam stood. "Sure...sure." He started toward the door. "By the way, what do you keep in that locked storage room downstairs?"

Rhoades blanched. "Nothing special. Some supplies."

"Like chemicals?" he asked, knowing he'd never get a truthful answer. "Call me as soon as you have the information I requested." He opened the door and strode out.

***

Although unsure of what to say to Frieda, who had left a couple of frantic messages hoping for news from Adam, he had to do what he could to comfort her. He clutched the wheel of his Jeep in anxious anticipation as he drove up to the Marquez house. Greeted first by Gabby and Sal, he stooped to give Gabby a hug as he watched Frieda rush from the porch to his car.

Frieda glanced at the empty passenger seat. "Where is Elena? I was hoping you had found her."

He worried his bottom lip. "I'm not certain of her whereabouts yet, but I'm hot on the trail."

Frieda's face drooped, which tore at Adam's heart. He slung his arm around her shoulders. "Don't give up hope now. I have critical information that I believe will lead me to her."

"What information, *mijo*?"

Frieda had addressed him with an affection endearment, and it touched him and galvanized his determination to find Elena, fast. "I don't want to get your hopes up, but I have reason to believe she might be with Ron."

"Ron? Why Ron?"

"I'm not certain, but I will check it out. Please keep this between us for now because if it is Ron, I don't want to tip him off that I'm onto him."

"Whatever you say," Arturo said, coming up behind Frieda. "We will do whatever you ask."

Adam shook Arturo's hand. "I have reported everything I know to the police and they're also looking into Elena's disappearance."

"Yes, we have heard from them."

"If they don't find her soon, I promise you, I will." As soon as the words escaped his lips he felt like a little kid telling a big fib. Did he really think he could find her before the cops?

He could only hope he could track her down, but even if he wasn't being totally truthful, his motivation was good. With all his heart, he wanted to reassure his adoptive family and, as much as possible, put them at peace. They were in enough pain and fear. All he could do was offer them some hope.

Frieda stared at him through tear-filled eyes. Despite her wrinkles, she looked like a lost child. "I know you will, *mijo*. You promised to return her to me and I believe you."

He hugged Frieda and crushed her to his chest, feeling tears soak his shoulder. "I'll do everything in my power to return her as soon as I can."

And he meant it.

Chapter 22

After returning to his quaint casita behind a larger stucco and frame house to shave and change his clothes, Adam went online seeking information on Ron. Although Frieda had nothing specific, an information and background service had no problem locating Ron's address and phone number.

Adam wrote it down, then struggled through LA traffic to Ron's house in Glendale. Adam knocked on the door, stirring up a commotion on the other side, and he heard a shout asking him to identify himself. When he answered, Ron told him to wait a moment.

Moments later, Ron cracked the door enough to step outside and quickly closed it behind him, not affording Adam a chance to glance inside.

"What are you doing here?" Ron asked suspiciously.

"Sorry to show up unexpectedly," Adam said, insincerely, "But I didn't have a chance to make plans. I don't know if you've been informed, but Elena is missing and hasn't been seen for a couple of days. We're concerned about her and wanted to ask if you might know anything."

Ron narrowed his eyes. "We?"

"I've been in contact with the family and they gave me permission to try and locate her."

Ron studied the ground as though there was something worthwhile written in the dirt. "Now, why would you think I have a clue about Elena? She rarely speaks to me, let alone tells me her itinerary."

Ron's attempt at lack of concern for Elena's welfare made Adam all the more suspicious. "I thought you might know something or would at least be worried about her."

"Of course I want to know if she's all right, but I have nothing to do with her disappearance and I don't like you implying that I do."

158

While Adam was pretty certain he had kept the edge out of his voice and attitude out of his gestures or features, Ron was intuitive enough to have picked up on Adam's suspicions. "I didn't intend to suggest anything of the sort. I'm worried about Elena and I'm seeking all possible help in locating her."

Ron's face softened. "Of course. Of course. I'm in shock. I'll do whatever I can to help you out."

"Right now, you can keep your eyes and ears open. If you hear or see anything that would be helpful in finding her, I'd like to know right away."

"Sure...sure. How do I get in touch with you?"

Adam handed him a card with his office number crossed out. "Here's my cell. Call me day or night." Although he doubted Ron ever would.

***

As soon as Adam had driven a mile away from Ron's house he pulled over and dialed Herman's number. After three rings, Herman answered.

"Herman, I need your help."

"Whatsup, boss? Do yuse know what happened to Elena?"

Adam wished. "Not exactly, but I have my suspicions. I visited Ron today. His behavior was so odd, I have a feeling he might know something more than he's admitting."

Herman snorted. "From what the guys told me, sounds like he's one oddball anyways."

Herman had a point, but it didn't quiet Adam's uneasiness. "Maybe, but I need to go into the house and see if I can find anything."

"Hows about calling the police?"

"I did, but they said they can't do anything other than follow the leads."

"Hows about a search warrant for Ron's house like they shows on TV?"

"I asked them about searching his house, but they said they'd need probable cause and all I have are suspicions. So unless I can get in there and come up with something substantial, we're out of luck." He hesitated. He had to convince Herman to take the risk. "I know

I'm asking a lot of you, but I have a plan. I'm going to give Ron a holler in a bit to tell him I believe someone at the power plant knows where she's at because we found something of hers there. I'm going to ask him to meet me after five at the security office."

Silence from Herman's end made Adam's heart race. Without Herman, this scheme was doomed.

Herman cleared his throat. "Okay, boss. What yuse want me to do?"

***

Adam parked his car down the street from Ron's house at the same time he was supposed to be meeting Ron at the plant. Herman would be doing the honors, equipped with a .45 pistol he kept for his own protection. His instructions were to keep Ron at the power plant until Adam conducted a search of Ron's house. Adam could only hope he would find something to make all the deception worthwhile. Otherwise, he would feel like a fool, and look like one, too, especially if later charged with breaking and entering.

He tried both the front and back doors, in case Ron had been careless. No such luck, but he couldn't help noticing the multi-pane windows, which could be readily opened if he broke out one small pane. He wrapped a small rock with a towel from his trunk and smashed a side window with ease, then snaked his arm through the opening, careful not to leave blood evidence, and then maneuvered the lock open. He lifted the window and crawled—leg, torso, head, leg—through the gap.

Once inside, he took a look around, surprised at how ordinary and orderly everything appeared. All was in its place. The desk in Ron's office was cleared of all clutter. The dishes were on a drain board in the kitchen sink. Even the knives were neatly stowed in a wooden block. He considered the condition of his own casita and smirked. This *was* unusual for a single man.

He went from room to room, noting that nothing was out of place, until he came upon the last bedroom at the end of the hallway and turned the knob. It was locked.

He tried again with the same result, then leaned his head against the door and asked, "Elena, are you in there?"

Although he heard no response, he repeated his question a couple more times while keeping an ear to the door. He could swear he heard a muffled scraping sound coming from the other side.

***

Elena could hardly believe her ears when she heard Adam's voice outside the bedroom. She had given up hope anyone would discover her whereabouts and rescue her from this hellish imprisonment. And yet, here was Adam, only feet away.

With her mouth taped and her hands tied, she had to move the chair to create a noise loud enough to alert him to her presence. She shifted her body weight to turn the chair, but it barely moved, the sound so muted she doubted he would hear her on the far side of the door.

Her heart pounded hard against her ribs and her palms sweated. She had to make her presence known. She jerked up in her seat and the chair scraped the wood floor with a distinctive sound. She repeated her action again and again, but she heard nothing more. She began to cry in frustration and anguish, but even her sobs were silenced by the tape. Adam hadn't heard her.

She might never be rescued, and from whatever his intention was in kidnapping her.

Chapter 23

At hearing the scraping sound, Adam knew exactly what he had to do. Since he had locked himself out of the car a couple of years earlier, he always carried a Slim Jim wedged securely between the Jeep's frame and body. He couldn't have used it on the deadbolts, but this was different. He could try it on a bedroom lock.

He rushed out to the Jeep and returned to poke the Slim Jim between the door and frame, jiggling the lock until he felt it shift. He swung the door open, hoping this wasn't a trap, and found a horrifying sight: Elena tied to a chair and gagged. As relieved as he was to see her alive, a red film coated his eyes and he body began to shake with rage.

His eyes locked on hers, which filled with tears as he made his way to her side. "I'm here, honey. I'm here. Everything's going to be all right." He kissed her forehead then told her, "I'm sorry. This is going to hurt." He tore the tape off of her mouth and extracted the wad of paper inside.

Elena gasped and then whispered, "You saved me."

***

As soon as Adam untied her hands from the chair, Elena threw her arms around his neck. He pressed her to his chest and held her there. Reluctant to let him go, she held onto him as she would a life preserver in turbulent seas.

When he finally released her, she asked, "How did you find me?"

"I've been searching for you for days, everywhere I could think of. Of course I was suspicious of the power company because it seemed they had more reason to want to shut you up. I never even considered it might be Ron. A tip from your buddy Herman led to finding your appointment book, then to discovering that Ron had participated in your *release* from Valley Hill. What happened?"

"When I went to take another water sample at the oil/water separator, I was picked up by security and held at their offices until Ron came to fetch me. I have no idea how he knew I was there, but since he works for the company, he must have been keeping tabs on my activities. Perhaps his unexpected gift-bearing visit was somehow connected to a prior arrangement to take me off their hands."

Adam turned a shade of red she had never seen before. "Those sons of bitches." He clenched his fists and his knuckles turned white. "What do you think Ron would have done with you?"

Elena quivered with the thought. "I don't know, but I'm glad you tracked me down before I had a chance to find out."

He placed his hand over hers. "I'm so grateful I found you." His eyes filled with tears. "I didn't want to lose you. I couldn't figure out how I could live without you. You've become—"

She pulled him to her and kissed him with all the love and gratitude her heart held. He returned her affection with an urgency she had never known. When he lifted his lips from hers, she told him, "I can't figure out how I'd live without you."

"You'll never have to because I will always be in your life, until death do us part."

***

Adam took Elena's hand as they approached the Marquez house. She quivered with excitement in his. She was going home. After filing a police report in LA, which took forever since detectives questioned her and Adam for a couple of hours, they made their way back to Vandasillo. On the ride home, Adam had her call the local PD to give them the report number filed with LAPD. Then she called Herman and told him the local police were on their way to pick up Ron.

"Yuse okay?"

"I am now. Thank you for everything you've done for me."

"Gotta make it up somehow."

When she laid the phone on her knee, Adam reached for her hand. "You all right?"

She nodded. She was more than all right. She was going home with Adam, who would always be there for her.

Before they reached the patio, Frieda and the rest of the Marquez clan surrounded them, and Adam watched as they extracted Elena, and bundled her into their arms. Surrounded by love and safekeeping, she beamed at him and jokingly complained, "Now look what you've done."

Frieda grabbed Adam's hand. "*Mijo*. You kept your promise."

"I have one more promise to keep. I'll be back soon."

Elena looked perplexed. "Where are you going?"

"I have one more thing to take care of. When security picked you up at the plant, had you successfully gathered more water samples, right?"

Elena grinned as she reached into her bra and produced a vial of water. "This is all I was able to hide from them in a hurry. They took the other two containers."

"Have it tested as soon as you can, although I suspect you'll get the same results as before. I know what I need to do. Wait here until I return. You're safe now."

He began to head back to the Jeep when she grabbed his bicep. "Where are you going?"

"Back to the plant. I'm not finished there yet."

"No." She shook her head. "Not without me."

He took her hand. "I have to do this alone. Ron is being held in security. I have to find out what he knows before the cops pick him up. You know he'll never talk in front of you."

Elena blanched. "*Dios mio.* I don't want you to go alone and put yourself in danger."

"Actually, as of now, I hold all the cards. I'm safe, but I need to know you're safe, too or I won't be able to do what I need to."

"Promise me you won't do anything foolish. Ron is more dangerous than he looks."

Adam tensed, knowing she was right, but not wanting to feed her fear. "I know that. I promise." He placed her hand in Frieda's. "Take care of my Elena while I'm gone."

Frieda smiled. "I will, *mijo*. I promise."

"I'll hold you to it."

***

Elena's heart shattered into a thousand pieces as she watched Adam drive away. She tried to pull her hand free of Frieda's, but her mother held on tightly and wouldn't let her go. A sob escaped her lips.

Frieda wrapped her in her arms. "Let him go, *mija*. He has to do this himself."

She strained in Adam's direction, but the longer Frieda held onto her the weaker she became, her knees buckling.

"You need to sit." Frieda led her on shaky legs to a patio chair where she was finally able to break down and weep after the sleepless and harrowing torment of her last few days.

Frieda stayed with her until the tears subsided, then left to bring her back a handful of tissues. "You need to rest. This has been hard on you."

She gazed up at her mother's wrinkled face framed by the late afternoon sunlight. "I will when Adam returns. Right now, I couldn't sleep if I tried. I'm too worried about him."

Frieda sighed then nodded. "Okay, *mija*, what can I do to make you more comfortable?"

"Go fetch me a cup of your fabulous coffee. I haven't had any in three days."

Frieda patted her hand. "Whatever you need, you let me know."

Even after everything she'd been through, Elena couldn't help smiling up at her mother, who at that moment looked like a saint with a sunlit halo.

Chapter 24

Adam stopped by his casita to draft two short documents before speeding over to the entrance of the power plant. From there he called Herman, who spoke with the guard and gained him entry.

Once inside the security suite, he located the office where Herman was holding Ron. Adam had to bury his fury. He couldn't let this bastard know Elena had been rescued and that the police were on the way to arrest him. Before Ron went away for a long, long time, Adam had to secure the information he needed from a director of operations at Valley Hill Gas and Electric.

Adam made his presence known with a cough. Herman met him at the door.

"Come on in, boss." He gestured toward a seated Ron who looked nervous and uncomfortable. "Ron's been waitin' for yous."

Adam walked up to Ron and it took everything in him not to beat the SOB bloody. "Sorry we had to detain you, but I had no choice."

"What the fuck," Ron said. "I've been here over five hours. You're wasting my time."

"But I haven't wasted mine." Adam pulled a chair up to Ron's. "I've been busy doing some research."

"What are you talking about?" Ron looked annoyed.

"Listen," Adam said. "I know Elena tried to talk to you about the contamination, but that you blew her off. Since then, we've learned a lot of about what's going on out here, and I have a document you need to sign. Read it over. It states that it has come to your attention there have been chemicals used by the power plant that have inadvertently contaminated the local water supply and, as the Director of Operations at Valley Hill, you agree to spend whatever money and resources are necessary to do a thorough cleanup. If you read further down, it states that the EPA will be involved in measuring the levels of all toxic chemicals before and after the cleanup."

Ron threw the paper on the floor. "How the hell can I sign this? I'm not the CEO."

Adam scooped up the form. "No problem. We'll inform the EPA, who are coming to do their own investigation, that you knew about the problems, ignored them, and told Elena all about it, but laughed it off."

Ron's mouth dropped open. "That's a lie."

"How would they know that? We have water samples and independent tests to back up our position. You, on the other hand, kidnapped your ex-wife and left her tied to a chair with tape over her mouth."

Ron swallowed hard. "Okay...wait a minute. Let me think."

"There's not much to think about. You sign this document, or you'll have more than kidnapping charges to deal with. There are people in this community with life-threatening diseases, all of which can be traced back to Valley Hill's negligence. How about we lay that all at your feet?"

"Okay. Shit. Okay."

Adam removed a pen from his pocket and flicked it, holding it out to Ron. He stared at the pen for a long moment before reaching for it. "You've given me no choice."

Exactly his intention.

***

Adam maneuvered his Jeep up the gravel drive to the Marquez house. Since leaving the power plant he'd had a perpetual smile on his face. On his way out, the police were headed in to arrest Ron.

Adam had done what he set out to do. He had protected the woman he loved, and at the same time performed a significant service for the community. For *his* community. Elena would be pleased with him. They had become a team in more ways than one.

During the night, while waiting in Rhodes's office, Adam had come to a decision that felt right, and necessary. This valley needed an advocate who would support *all* of the community's needs. He'd hang out a shingle and start his own law firm. Even though he knew he'd starve for a while, but he had the unique prospective of knowing how Valley Hill worked from the inside. Any lawsuits brought against the company would be in good hands with their former counsel.

He pulled to a stop not far from the covered patio. Gabby was the first one to race up to the Jeep, followed by Sal. Behind them tottered Frieda with the help of Arturo, who had her by the arm. Adam climbed out and was quickly surrounded by the Marquez family...his family.

Since meeting them, and seeing what real warmth and family meant, confirmed what he'd felt for years: he had never bonded with his own family. His parents had been unavailable physically and emotionally. They were too busy with their own lives to participate in his or pay attention to him. That explained his hunger to be a part of a close-knit family, and why, without looking at who Brittany really was, he'd jumped without thinking into proposing marriage. Being with Elena and her family, he knew the Marquez family were the family he had always wanted.

He hugged Frieda and Gabby, and shook Arturo's outstretched hand.

Frieda looked him over as though she was expecting bruises. "Are you okay, *mijo*? We were worried about you."

"I'm fine. More than fine. I'm great."

Adam turned around then asked, "Where's Elena? I want to tell you what happened at the same time."

Frieda made a face. "She waited on the patio a long time for you to return, but she was exhausted. She felt dirty and I made her take a bath. I told her I would wait for you while she soaked."

Adam smiled. "Good for you. But would you mind if I were to fetch her? I'd like her to be with us when I tell you about Ron."

"You go, Adam," Frieda said. "Go bring her into the kitchen. I make a fresh pot of coffee and I have *churros* for us all."

Everyone accompanied Adam into the house, but when he turned down the hall, Frieda, Arturo, Gabby and Sal made their way into the kitchen. "I'm not sure which room is hers," he said over his shoulder.

"The last one the left," Frieda called.

He found the room, but the door was closed. He knocked gently. Elena swung opened the door and yelped, "Adam," then threw herself at him. He wrapped her up in his arms and held her tight.

"I have good news for you," he whispered in her ear. "You won't have to worry about Ron anymore." He told her what had happened, and that the best-case scenario for Ron was he'd be in prison for six to eight years.

She pulled back and looked up, relief clear in her expression. "I don't know how to thank you enough. I never expected this result. You're the best lawyer, lover, man, a woman could have."

He kissed her with all the love and joy he held in his heart.

Through Elena and her love, he saw himself in a new light and gained a whole new respect for himself, a whole new reason to live.

They remained in each other's arms until Gabby came rushing down the hall to find them. "Coffee's ready," she said breathlessly, "and *Abuela* wants you in the kitchen right away. She says she can't wait much longer to hear Adam explain what happened."

Elena smiled up at him. "*Mi madre* has spoken. We shouldn't keep her in suspense."

Adam took her hand in his and laced their fingers. "It's time to join the family."

Together they walked hand and hand down the hall and into their future.

ABOUT THE AUTHOR

J. K. Winn has many stories to share. After years of working in the real world, including practicing psychotherapy and teaching at the college level, she decided to reinvent herself midlife to pursue her love of story.

She has six previously published novels, a play produced by the Actor's Alliance of San Diego, and poetry anthologized in *The Love of Writing* by the San Diego Writer's Workshop. Her play *Gotcha!* was selected for a reading at the Village Arts Theater in Carlsbad, California.

She lives by the beach in San Diego County, California.

CONNECT WITH J.K.
Website: jkwin.com
Instagram: @authorjkwinn
Facebook: authorjkwin
Twitter: @authorjkwinn
LinkedIn: j-k-winn

www.BOROUGHSPUBLISHINGGROUP.com

If you enjoyed this book, please write a review. Our authors appreciate the feedback, and it helps future readers find books they love. We welcome your comments and invite you to send them to info@boroughspublishinggroup.com. Follow us on Facebook, Twitter and Instagram, and be sure to sign up for our newsletter for surprises and new releases from your favorite authors.

Are you an aspiring writer? Check out www.boroughspublishinggroup.com/submit and see if we can help you make your dreams come true.

www.ingramcontent.com/pod-product-compliance
Lightning Source LLC
Chambersburg PA
CBHW051825170626
46807CB00003B/1033